BILLIE SOMEDAY

The Greatest of All Time

A NOVEL

ANDY GRAHAM

RIVER GROVE
BOOKS

Published by River Grove Books
Austin, TX
www.rivergrovebooks.com

Distributed by River Grove Books

Design and composition by Greenleaf Book Group
Cover design by Greenleaf Book Group
Cover images: ©ActiveLines, MicroOne, Wectors
used under license from Shutterstock.com

Publisher's Cataloging-in-Publication data is available.

Print ISBN: 978-1-63299-386-1

eBook ISBN: 978-1-63299-387-8

First Edition

For June, for your fearless and fierce attitude.

DARKWOOD
FOREST

THE
FARMER'S
HOUSE

THE
SCHOOLYARD
PEN

THE BARN

GROWNUP
PEN

BIG TRACTOR ROAD

Chapter 1

It may have felt like an ordinary July morning high in this mountain valley, but you can be sure that it was not. This was a special day, because in the valley there happened to be a farm where, on a barn floor of well-trampled hay and mud, a proud mother goat lay chewing a bit of cud, waiting to give birth. She was alone for the moment, but soon there would be a sweltering gale of commotion, including a farmer, a doctor, wet nurses, dry nurses, congratulators—and a handful of nosy goats that would begin prodding for details. They would be asking whether there were two newborn bucklings or two doelings or one of each. They would also want to know if the kids were healthy, the eye color, and the number of horns. Did the newborns have the customary four legs, or had something gone wrong? But for now, they left the first-time mother alone in her warm stable. If everything went according to plan, the new mother, Edna, just knew in her heart that she'd soon be nursing two beautiful kids.

Edna secretly hoped it would be two bucklings, and that another of her two greatest legacies in life would be fulfilled. She knew her purpose, and that was to have kids and provide her highly coveted milk to the farmer. Milk with enough fat in it to produce an endless supply to drink, make nutritious cheeses, and provide life-building energy. As she lay there on the mud chewing her cud, Edna was beaming with the sort of pride only a soon-to-be mother could boast.

"Make room, make room!" Doctor Sylvia cried out through the crowd of onlookers.

"How many, Doctor Sylvia? How many kids does she have?" a voice from the crowd impatiently shouted.

"I think I see the head," another voice rang out. "Yes, indeed, I do. It's got fine little nubs showing already!"

"That means it's a boy! Thank the heavens for that!" said a third doe.

"You have horns—that doesn't make you a buck, now, does it?" said the second doe.

"Doctor Sylvia, does he have all four legs? Where's the second kid?" another doe's voice was heard over those of the others.

"Quiet down, ladies. Give Edna time," Doctor Sylvia said calmly.

"There he is!"

"Here he comes!"

"He's going to be such a handsome thing!"

Doctor Sylvia's voice rose above the crowd's growing excitement, which was on the fringe of becoming out of control. "It's a girl! And it looks like there is only one!"

The crowd gasped and sighed its disappointment as the does further trampled the already well-trampled floors on the way out of the stable.

"Edna, my dear, what have you decided to name her?" the doctor asked, unaffected by the other goats' disappointment.

"I was so sure I was going to have bucklings. I was planning to name one of them Billy and the other James," Edna replied.

"Then Billie it is, but with an -*ie* at the end of her name," Doctor Sylvia said.

"I like that . . . Billie. Billie. What do you think about that, Billie?" Billie was trying to stand up on her own, but her mother's strong tongue kept knocking her down before she could maintain her balance for even a split second. Surely she'd be clean as a whistle before she ever stepped one hoof outside the stable.

Billie's grandmother Sappho peeked into the stable just as the commotion from nosy goats settled down in the birthing area. "She's going to like that name just fine, Doc," Sappho said. "Billie is a beautiful name for a beautiful girl, and this proud grandmother is going to help raise her to be a fantastic little goat." Sappho got closer to her granddaughter so she could see her little face. "Welcome to the world, Billie. May you be the greatest of us all." She turned and faced her own daughter, Edna, who had just grown up and fulfilled her dream in front of her eyes. "Edna, you've done a fine job. Bond with her now while you can, for soon you'll be separated."

The farmer stepped into the barn for a moment to see how his latest mother was faring. Satisfied by what he saw, he grinned, walked out of the stable, and left the new mother alone to do what she was born to do.

Chapter 2

As the close of September neared, the last of the summer heat escaped their little mountain farm, and the morning dew was hinting at becoming morning frost sooner rather than later. Billie's mother was out doing her duty on the grazing hill, and that duty was to make milk out of the most nutritious kinds of cud she could find. Without a doubt, the highlands contained the finest grazing areas, so Edna was off on a grazing adventure that Billie could only imagine. This was because Billie was being safely fenced in with the other kids on the farm, almost completely guarded from the dangers of the outside world. In fact, the only things they could see from their pen were the schoolyard stable on one side, the farmer's log cabin on the other, Big Tractor Road out front, and the Darkwood Forest looming behind them.

That was Billie's whole world, or at least what she knew of it by sight. The only evidence that the world was bigger than that was either from stories she had listened to or from noises she could hear from far-off places beyond her pen. For example, from time to time she could hear her mother calling to her even though she was out of view. When Edna's check-up calls came, Billie imagined what the world looked like through her mother's eyes. Other times she heard a strange creature shouting "moooooo" at them from the far side of the stable. The noise always seemed to be paired with the deep gongs of a bell. She wondered what that creature with the bell looked like. One day, the farmer's work dog, Caesar, was walking by on his way to get the adults from off the grazing hill when the "moo" sound happened again. Billie asked him about it. He stopped and replied, "It's just the cow, mate. She's nothing to fret over. What you and the other kids need to be afraid of is them howlers over in Darkwood. Those howls come from bunyips you never wanna see with your own eyes, mate. Those blokes live all over the forest, so steer clear of it, ya hear?"

"What's a bunyip?" Billie asked.

"It's a bunyip . . . a beast, mate. They're the ones that howl. Beasts, I tell ya," he replied as he trotted off.

Billie remembered hearing those howls. Some days, the howls were shouted across the farm from all directions. The notion of these bunyips made the kids shudder. The schoolyard stable area usually felt safe—that is, unless one of the kids found themselves drifting too close to the looming forest. If that happened, the secure feeling their pen offered during recess would suddenly vanish, a cold tingle would shiver down their spines, and play-time was over. Once the whole group of kids secured a spot safely away from the woods again, they could begin the process of calming down.

The shadowy woodland just loomed back there. No one on the farm ever seemed to actually enter it for any reason whatso-ever, not even Caesar. It was always dark, always mysterious, and hovered over the farm eternally. Ignoring its presence was consid-ered best practice for the farm goats because whether you were five days old or five thousand, the act of walking into its shadows was expressly forbidden.

Billie was just three months old now but was growing more

and more fearless. She was certainly unafraid of any dangers she found inside their little enclosed environment. None of the doelings or bucklings she lived with were quite as fearless as she was, and the other kids knew it. They regularly dared her into trying increasingly dangerous stunts. Though the dares were becoming increasingly difficult, she never refused any of them. There were three little bucklings in the schoolyard stable, and more often than not, it was one of them challenging her into the dares. There were four little does as well, but Billie spent far less time with them. Ovid was her closest friend of the bunch, but Virgil and Homer were good pals as well.

Homer was a sturdy-looking buckling with wide white haunches, a thick brown neck, and a poised brown face, quite the specimen. He was always trying to make up stories about going on adventures or off to battle some enemy, as if war was the only true way to learn about yourself.

Virgil was a tall buckling with brown hair going from his hooves to his knees. Above the knees, he had longer white hair growing from his haunches all the way up. He also had tremendously long ears that helped him hear the important details in stories that might have been missed by the others listening to the same tale. He kept a tally of those details so he could weave them into his own stories later on. It bears mentioning twice: Virgil was very tall. He was as tall as Billie's mother, Edna, at only a few months of age. There was no doubt that when he grew up, he'd tower over every goat on the farm.

As impressive as the other two bucklings' attributes were, most of Billie's time was occupied with her closest friend, Ovid. He was undersized when compared to most of the others, but what he lacked in size he made up for with his huge imagination. He was always sharing his imaginative tales with whoever was willing to listen. Billie was usually his victim because, ofttimes, she was trapped in some gutsy maneuver or concentrating on another death-defying act whenever he decided it was time to share. Everyone in the schoolyard but Ovid would explode with excitement when Billie performed her tricks, but when they got excited, Ovid would only become overly concerned, or distracted by some physical element involved in her stunt.

The four doelings Billie lived with were all white and had fine, soft hair. They seemed to really love that about themselves. Their love of hair was pretty obvious because they were regularly keeping it straight or clean, and if they weren't doing that, they were talking about it. Maya was their leader, and her two best friends, Phillis and Emily, were always tagging along somewhere behind her. They always stayed close so they were ready to take whatever Maya said and run with it some more. Kate was smallest of the four white doelings, and Maya's crew went back and forth trying to decide whether or not to treat Kate as one of them. Kate had a mind of her own though, and Maya found that kind of quality to be non-best-friend material.

"Billie, you've climbed the *tire tower*, and now you must fling yourself down while hoping for the mercy of gravity's will. What part of you thought this was a good idea?" Ovid asked the daredevil.

"The part that knows that *someday* I'll be the greatest of all time, Ovid!" Billie finished her sentence and casually leapt over headfirst to a red pile of dirt that was just within reach. She tumbled down its slope, and when she came to a rolling stop, she was facing her friend.

The cheers sounded from the others: "NICE! Sweet jump, Billie! Good one!" But Ovid was unmoved.

"This dirt pile . . . ," Ovid mused. "What faraway place did it come from? It has a dark red hue to it that simply does not match the soil we have in our pen. How did it get here, I wonder?"

"I don't know, Ovid," Billie replied. "I just jumped toward the pile because it was there."

"Yes, but why is it there, and where did it come from? This is an important element of our narrative. It's part of the story of why we've come to live with the things we live with inside our fences," Ovid asked again, unsatisfied.

"I don't know. Maybe it came from some piece of land down the road with red dirt, I'm guessing?" Billie tried to satisfy him.

"Yes, the Redlands. Yes, Billie, indeed. Too many bad things must've happened in the Redlands, so the farmer left that place and brought a token of that memory with him. A token brought with him from his previous land that was stained *red* by bloody trials he survived while living in that inhospitable place. The red pile is our reminder to work hard and fend off those that would seek to hurt us. Those that reign in the Darkwood Forest . . . and beyond." Ovid invented all kinds of unnecessary details, being the bag of wind that he was.

Homer interceded from behind the tire tower. "There's nothing dangerous enough in Darkwood that it can't be outsmarted, outfought, or waited out. I'd be made king of the forest if I ever adventured out into those trees." He paused. "But bravo for your latest trick. That was really something, Billie!"

"*Don't* go near that forest, kids!" Caesar barked at them from the farmer's porch. "Trust me, mates, there's things in there that would even scare the farmer. You go in there and . . ."

"And what, Caesar?" Billie challenged the Australian shepherd. "You've never once told us what's really out there."

"You don't wanna know," he barked. "Have a sleep, kids. That's enough for today."

"But, Caesar, we haven't even had milk yet," Maya, the oldest doeling, cried out.

"The farmer'll bring it before dark," Caesar told her.

"Yeah, but it's not even time for dark," Virgil said.

Caesar answered quickly, "Winter's coming soon. Days get shorter, and my fuse does too. Just listen to me and stay away from the woods. Do exactly as you're told." With that said, he went around the schoolyard stable to begin his last herding duty for the day.

When Caesar was just out of earshot, Homer looked around, then spoke up. "I dare you to go into Darkwood Forest, little miss thinks-she's-the-greatest-of-all-time."

"Don't listen to him, Billie," Ovid warned.

"When?" Billie asked, accepting the dare right away.

"Tomorrow. Right after Caesar goes to fetch our moms," Homer instructed. "You have to go in, fetch a good stone as proof you were there, then come back out with it. Simple."

"All right then. Tomorrow."

The date for Billie's dare was set.

Chapter 3

"**G**ood morning, Billie Someday. Are you ready for your last performance ever?" Homer chirped at Billie before the rooster even had a chance to announce the arrival of the morning sun. He must've woken up early to rib her a little before the big day, but this was the first time anyone had ever called her "Billie Someday."

"I was born that way, Homer," said Billie.

"Which way is that?" asked Homer.

"Born ready. But it won't be my final feat. Not even close," Billie said with complete confidence. She paused, then asked, "Why did you call me Billie Someday?"

"You said it yourself, you know—*someday* you'll be the greatest of all time." Homer looked over in the direction of where they were the day before, then back at Billie. "Remember?"

"Yeah, well . . . I will be."

Ovid said, "Go back to sleep, Billie. It's story day, then you have the big stunt afterward, so save your energy. You'll need it to fight off the monsters in Darkwood."

Billie lay there trying to get some sleep, but her thoughts about the near future kept her brain busy. She was trying to weave the various scenarios of the soon-to-come daredevil show in her imagination, but found herself thinking about story day as well. All goats love a good story, and story day was led by one of her favorite beings on the farm, her grandmother. After fantasizing for a while and without getting a wink of shuteye, Billie heard the rooster announce daybreak. "Errrr-ur-err-ur-errrrrr!" She heard the gates open up to the grownup goat barn, then she heard the farmer begin to milk the mothers one by one. Milking time was always chatter time between the mothers and their kids. Edna and Billie's chatter opportunity was no different this morning.

"How are you doing, sweetheart?" Edna asked Billie. "How was schoolyard yesterday?"

"I'm fine, Mama," Billie answered. "No need to worry over me. Yesterday Virgil dared me to climb the tire tower, and so I did. To get down, I jumped over to the red dirt pile and rolled out of my fall. It was awesome, but I can probably do better if I hit the takeoff really hard next time."

"You know I don't like it when you take risks. You make me nervous all day with stories like that. You're going to hurt yourself if you're not careful. Then where would you be? They'd take you away from me and put you someplace where I wouldn't be able to help. That's where you'd be."

"It was no big deal. I was fine. I know what I'm doing."

"Billie, I just want you to be safe. You should spend more time on the ground thinking about your actual future and less time with your head up in the clouds dreaming about dares." She paused. "Today is your grandmother's story day, so I expect you to be on your best behavior. She works hard on those stories, so I want you to pay attention. Don't go off and break anything. Not today . . . or ever."

"Yes, Mama."

Edna said, "Ovid's mama is next, so be a good little doeling and go fetch him."

"Yes, ma'am."

Billie walked over to Ovid. "My mama said you're up next." She traded places with the buckling, then looked over the back fence at Darkwood. No one was paying attention to what she was doing after the conversation with her mother, so she just gave the shadowy forest a stare down to test her courage. She could feel little tingles in her spine building and fear growing inside her as she peered into the woods. She wanted to look away but couldn't pull her gaze from that ominous forest on the backside of their farm. She gathered her fears that had built up so that they were all in one place, and she pushed them back down to where they came from.

"There are so many eyes in there, and they're always watching. The trick is to find theirs before they find yours, kid."

Billie looked around to see where the strange voice was coming from but couldn't see any strangers. The voice repeated itself, but louder this time. "I said, the trick is finding their eyes before they find yours."

Her heart started racing like crazy as she looked around in panic. Two distinct choices took over her mind, and they were both purely instinctual. *Fight or flight?*

The voice said, "Don't move an inch." Billie could feel something soft and furry curling between her two hind legs. She tensed her legs and started to kick.

Chapter 4

"**D**on't do that! Please don't do that!" the strange voice said hurriedly, as Billie kicked as hard as she possibly could. Fortunately, her hooves had made absolutely no contact with the chatty creature.

"*Goodnight*, kid! You've got Zeus powers in that kick, don't you?" The voice was off to her side now.

Billie turned to see a creature she'd never seen before.

"Hahahahaha!" Billie's knees collapsed, and she rolled over onto her back in laughter. When she stopped laughing, she asked, "What are you?"

"I'm an Antoni," the cat said.

"What's an Antoni?" Billie asked.

"It's me—it's my name," she replied. "I'm Antoni, the farm cat." Antoni was still breathing heavily from the narrowly avoided hoof attack.

"Well, Antoni, why'd you sneak up on me if you scare so easily?" Billie asked with a smirk. She was looking at a longhaired gray cat with a bushy tail staring back at her with panicked golden eyes. The wide-eyed feline had triangular gray ears with black lines marking their edges and long hairs protruding from their points. In fact, the cat's whole body was full of long black lines that added a sharpness to its already beautiful appearance.

"I don't know. I saw a steady pair of legs and thought I'd figure-eight them," Antoni huffed with the limited air she had in her breath.

"What's that?"

"Stand up and I'll show you, *but* . . . you have to promise *not* to kick me."

"I promise. Cross my hooves and hope to die, stick a hay needle in my eye," Billie said as she got up on all fours. Antoni began a cautious walk toward the little doeling. As Antoni got closer, she paused to stretch out her front legs, then sat down and stared off at the top of the schoolyard stable, clearly distracted by some unknown object up there. Billie waited a while, then decided to ask, "Whatcha looking at so intensely?"

"Something moved," Antoni chirped.

"What moved?" Billie asked.

"Something. Quit asking silly questions—I don't know yet," said Antoni, then moved closer to Billie, cocked her head, and began straightening the hair on Billie's haunches with a rough tongue.

"What are you doing now?" Billie asked.

"You're a complete mess." Antoni continued grooming her.

As Ovid finished speaking with his mother, he looked over and saw what was going on with Billie. Seeing what looked like the cat gnawing at Billie's leg, Ovid immediately charged the unknown creature with his head lowered, and he had intent to harm. As Ovid charged the stranger, he shouted, "Leave my friend alone, creep!"

Noticing Ovid's assault, Antoni leapt high into the air without a sound, and she timed her jump perfectly. Ovid's horns missed completely. As the cat dropped back down, she aimed for Billie's back and landed on it gracefully. She made sure she was balanced first, then checked herself for injuries. "Perhaps figure eights will have to wait for a day more suited for the civilized," she said from her new perch.

"Let her be, Ovid," Billie said. "She's friendly."

"Perhaps you could safely direct our conversation toward that fence so I may retire to safer pastures?" Antoni said regally from the safety of Billie's back. Billie obliged, and as soon as the fence was close enough, Antoni leapt effortlessly to the top rail. Again she established her balance, but this time it was on the split pine log of the top fence rail.

"Come on, Billie, leave that tomcat be," Ovid said.

"She's not a tomcat. She's an Antoni-cat," Billie said.

"How do you know it's a she?" Ovid asked.

"I don't know how I know. I just *know*," Billie replied. "Antoni is a girl."

"Yeah, well, she's got a boy's name."

Billie turned her back to Ovid, then replied to her friend, "Yeah, well, so do I, and it never changed who I am." She continued walking toward the schoolyard stable for story time.

Antoni shouted toward the departing goats, "You've got good instincts, kid! Catch you later. And, Ovid, feel free to find a moment to relax! The whole world isn't after you, or your friends, contrary to your belief. If you could see that, surely you'd be open to the possibility of our friendship. I'm simply asking for a chance here!"

Ovid stopped and yelled back, "I'll give you a chance at my horns, if you like chances so much."

"You two stop," Billie commanded.

Ovid lowered his voice and replied, "I'll stop, but only because it's Sappho's story time." He turned and walked toward the barn.

Billie turned back to Antoni. "See you later, Antoni!"

"Later, sugar cube."

"Perhaps next time we'll have a more harmonious interaction?" Billie said.

"Harmony is overrated, kid. Balance is where it's at."

Chapter 5

Sappho waited for the kids to enter the schoolyard barn, her head held high as she counted the walk-ins. "Come on in, Virgil—pick a spot over here by the hay bale. Maya, you and your friends should have plenty of space right there. Welcome, Homer, come on in. You can lay yourself down over in that space with the straw piled there. Ovid, sweetheart, you too. Now where's my Billie?" Sappho asked her story-time guests.

"She's coming, Miss Sappho. She was talking to that big furball."

"There she is." Sappho spoke louder and pointed her voice toward the entrance so Billie could hear her. "And how was our farm cat doing today?"

"She's great, Grandma. I really like her!" Billie replied.

"She's nothing but a hairy pile of trouble," Ovid said sharply.

"Yes, Antoni is hairy, but most cats are. And if you haven't noticed yet, she does plenty of good for this farm. For instance, have you been sick even once in your life, Ovid?" Sappho asked.

"No, ma'am."

"Well, that's because Antoni keeps the mice away, and mice carry all kinds of invisible trouble with them, like the goatbonic plague. So you be nice to her, Ovid. Thank her for your good health next time you get the chance."

"Yes, ma'am," Ovid said as Billie walked over and nestled up to him for story time.

"You miss me, Ovid?" Billie teased her friend in a whisper, careful not to disrupt the beginning of the coveted story time.

Ovid playfully furrowed his brow back at her but was ultimately focused on Sappho.

"Well, which story shall I tell you today? 'The Goat Who Cried Coyote' or 'The Little Goat That Could'? How about 'Randolph the Red-Nosed Billy Goat'? 'E.B.'s Web'?" Sappho looked around the stable and paused after each story she mentioned to gauge the crowd's interest.

Homer spoke up. "I want a scary one."

"A scary one . . . hmm? Has anyone ever told you about *wolves*?" Sappho asked with a seriousness on her face that none of them had seen before.

"No, ma'am," Homer said.

Sappho's seriousness remained unchanged. "Then I'll tell you the tale of 'The Wolf and the Hare.' Long ago, up on a bountiful grazing hill not far from here, on the first day of winter's end, the snow had melted, and a lovely young hare poked its head out from the safety of its burrow. The hare was very hungry and hadn't eaten much during the winter months, so she went foraging on the hills. The hare foraged until she was full, but she got greedy and wanted more. Looking around at the wide-open fields, she noticed an area near Darkwood Forest where she hadn't foraged before."

"Don't do it, hare," Maya, the oldest doeling, murmured.

"Maya's right. The hare should not have gone anywhere near Darkwood Forest, and the hare knew that too, but the hare's stomach kept telling her *more, more, more*, so she went anyway. She headed right toward the Darkwood Forest and started eating. There was tons to eat at the edge of the forest, so the rabbit just ate and ate and forgot where she was. Just as she grew comfortable with her surroundings, a wolf spotted her from within the forest. It had been a long winter for the wolf as well, so he was hungry too. The big wolf got low to the ground and crept closer to the hare, little by little, only moving when the hare was looking away so that he couldn't be detected. His long hair lay flat so his scent wouldn't be picked up on the wind and warn the rabbit of his presence. His sharp teeth were ready to snap down on that hare's spine, but he needed to wait for the best time to chase the rabbit. He kept his yellow eyes and both of his pointy ears focused in the hare's direction. When the hare turned its head away from the shadowy wood for just a split second, the wolf sprang into action. The chase was on. The hare spotted the wolf as it got close, and she did her best to put a little distance between herself and him. She started tiring, and the wolf was getting so close that she felt his every breath. The hare was just about to be caught, but she remembered how quickly she could change direction, so she did just that and started doing circles around the wolf. The wolf was fast and powerful, but all that power was useless on the agile hare out in the open. The hare got away."

"That doesn't sound scary," Billie said.

"That's not the end of the story, Billie," Sappho warned her granddaughter. "The next day the hare went to forage again. Remembering that there was so much more to eat near Darkwood, she returned to the scene, knowing she could run circles around the big bad wolf."

"Yeah, that doesn't really sound that scary, Miss Sappho," Ovid said.

"True, one wolf is not scary if you're as fast as a hare, but you're not a hare, are you? You can climb, jump, and gallop, and you've got horns. You can use them all to protect yourself, but no matter how fast you move your legs, you'll never have a hare's gift of speed to aid your escape. All that being said, this still isn't the moral of the story for the hare, Ovid. The moral of the story applies to all animals that encounter a wolf. The next day she went right back to the lush place near Darkwood and began to forage. Before she could take a single bite of the bountiful flora surrounding her, a whole pack of wolves came charging out of the woods. They had been waiting for her. She ran as fast as she could, but they spread out to chase her together as a team. At first, she thought she'd be able to outrun them, but wolves have stamina that can drive them to extremes when they're chasing their dinner. The wolves stayed close, chasing the hare until it reached a creek. The hare tried to run them in circles, but the wolves were too spread out. Her only chance was to make it back to her burrow and dive into the safety of her underground home. She headed toward the burrow, then thought better of it. Her little innocent rabbits lived there, and leading the wolves to her hidden home would be treacherous because wolves can dig very well. She turned and ran back toward Darkwood, moving into the danger and away from her loved ones. Seconds later, the wolves caught her, and she learned her lesson right then and there." Sappho had finished her story.

"What lesson did she learn, Grandma?" Billie asked.

"This is not a nice lesson with third and fourth chances, Billie. The hare was killed, torn to pieces." Sappho stared at them coldly, poised to deliver the cold truth. "The moral of the story is to never challenge the wolves and never go into Darkwood Forest. Don't even go *near* it. Wolves are real, and they're always looking for their next meal. Yes, I know they bring balance to nature, and there's nothing they're doing in the story that's bad. The wolves were just doing what wolves do. But you need to know that they can take advantage of the tiniest of mistakes that we animals make, so show them respect, and stay away from their forest. It is theirs, and they do not share it," Sappho explained. "Wolves aren't the only predators in there, either. There are cats twenty times the size of Antoni in there. Bears, badgers, foxes, birds of prey—they're all in there, and none of them are to be taken lightly. They all deserve our respect."

"Where did all those predators come from, Miss Sappho?" Ovid asked the storyteller.

"They came from our Mother."

Suddenly, Caesar came in through the stable doors with an announcement: "Story time's over, mates. No earbashing about it. You kids go have a bit of sunshine and some exercise. Sappho, you know the drill—get a cold drink for yourself, then back to the bush, mate."

Sappho made her way to the water trough, thirsty after the telling of the long tale. As she drank, she hoped her story emphasized the importance of staying far away from Darkwood.

Chapter 6

Sappho joined up again with the grownup goats up on the grazing hill. Meanwhile, the kids were back in the schoolyard pen, as always.

"What's wrong?" Ovid asked Billie. "You're kind of quiet."

"Nothing," she answered.

"You're worried about the big stunt later, aren't you?" Ovid asked.

"I'm not worried about anything. I'm just figuring out my plan."

"Billie, do you know where wolves come from?"

"Sappho said they come from our Mother, so they come from our Mother. No need to overthink it, Ovid."

Ovid was always looking to sharpen his storytelling skills after Sappho's story time, even though he wasn't the best at it. This time, he was focused on the origin of the predators in Darkwood. "All wolves were descendants of the most heinous goat to *ever* walk on a farm. One horrible day, that heinous goat started eating the most disgusting thing there is: *flesh*. It all started when the heinous goat ate his very own mother," Ovid said.

Antoni slipped out from behind Ovid and said, "What's wrong with eating flesh?"

"Yeah, what Antoni said. The type of food you eat shouldn't make you who you are. It's what you have inside you that counts . . . and I don't mean what's inside your stomach there, milk-buckling," Billie quipped.

"It matters if you eat your own mother." Ovid ignored them both. "That's why you always see wolves in a pack. They're like goats in how they like to stick together in a pack, because they were goats originally. That's the only goat part of them that's left, but they call themselves a pack rather than a herd. And so, when that heinous goat finished eating his mother's body, he ate her brains. When her brains were gone, he started bleating so loud the whole farm heard it, but his bleats quickly morphed into howls. The brains that goat ate . . . they *erased* its mind, and it became mad with the love of flesh. Now the wolves are all mindless savages that constantly hunt for innocent animals in the forest, howling all night, lusting over our brains."

Antoni quipped, "You're a fool if you think wolves are mindless. They work together all the time, and they howl to spread messages over huge stretches of land. They're dangerous, too. They don't need a farmer or anything to protect their pack. They don't need anything to protect themselves from danger. They don't need it because they *are* the danger, kid."

Ovid looked over at the cat and waited for her to stop with the unsolicited commentary before he continued. "We heard about them today. We know everything about them now. And they're not the only danger in the woods. Those little mice that you fail to find, Antoni, are the reason we have bears. They're the mice that grew *so* greedy and ate *so* much at the farm that they couldn't fit through the little holes and crevices around the stable anymore, *so* . . . they were forced to leave. They hopped the back fence, climbed up the slopes, and found great big caves where the biggest monsters all live. They became bears. Bears that could eat as much as they wanted and get as big as a tractor. All they had to do was live the easy life on the farm as mice, pick up scraps, and avoid our lazy cat, and they would have it made in our organized world, but instead, they're bears out in the wild now, and they have to work hard for all that extra food."

"Bears have been around a lot longer than I have, so blame the ancient cats . . . not me. They were way lazier than me," Antoni said, closing her eyes.

"Hey, Antoni, there goes another one!" Billie flicked her nose and pointed her eyes toward a mouse.

"Nah." Antoni stretched her front legs. "I'll get that one the day after tomorrow." She took two steps, repositioned herself, and lay back down in a sunny spot in the grass.

Suddenly, Virgil jumped up on a couple of stacked tires that were sitting behind them. He was inspired by Sappho's story day as well. He said, "This farm wasn't built in a day, but it could fall apart in one if everyone doesn't do their part."

"Here we go again, more stories." Billie laughed. "Bucklings always have their own stories after story time."

"Fine, I'll save that one for later then. You'll all want to know how the farm got organized into a superior society one of these days," Virgil remarked arrogantly.

"I wanna hear your story," Maya said, looking at Virgil. "Got any about star-crossed lovers, Virgil?"

"You kids quit wasting time," Homer declared as he watched the herd dog leave the farm gates. "Caesar just went around the stable, so now it's time for Billie's last hurrah!"

"Woohoo!" Virgil shrieked.

"You can do it!" Kate, the youngest and second smallest of all the doelings, cheered. Billie was the only doeling smaller than Kate.

Billie stopped and stared toward Darkwood for a moment to visualize her performance, then walked out in front of the kids. This prompted her audience to look beyond Billie at the forest behind her. She paced back and forth a few times, then started her presentation. "Does and bucks, bucklings and doelings, kids of all ages, it is my pleasure to present the 'Forbidden Forest Waltz,' where I, Billie Someday, will enter Darkwood, pick one beautiful round stone up off the forest floor, and bring that stone back to the farm, accomplishing all of this completely unscathed so I can live to tell the *whole* farm about it."

Billie silently paced back and forth for a while to build some tension in the hearts of her fellow stablemates. All the while, she looked them in the eye, one by one. "Virgil, Maya, Ovid. Please step forward." Virgil and Ovid got up right away and came forward. Maya was slower to get up from the comfort of her little patch of grass by her friends, but she made her way and joined the selected volunteers. Billie got into Virgil's face and looked him right in the eye. "Virgil, you are the tallest among us. Tell us, what do you see over the top of our back fence?" She was getting so close to Virgil that, intimidated by the combination of her advance and Darkwood Forest looming behind her, he started backing up.

Virgil replied, "I see the woods. They're dark. I can't really make anything out, but the trees are moving back and forth." Virgil had backed up so far now as a result of Billie's advance that he bumped up against the fence behind him. "Ouch!" He paused, then shared the last part of his description with a tremble in his voice. "Um . . . the woods look spooky and chaotic, just like they always do."

"Thank you for your assistance, Virgil. You stay right where you are." Billie moved back to where Maya and Ovid were waiting for each of their turns. This time she locked eyes with Maya. "Look at Darkwood Forest, Maya. What do you hear?"

Intimidated by the forest, Maya started backing up while she looked Billie in the eye.

"Look at Darkwood, not at me," Billie said. "Look through the fence, between the slats. Listen and tell me what you hear."

Maya backed into Virgil and shrieked, "Aieeeeee!" She turned and huddled closely with Virgil. Virgil's knees were knocking together and were as rattled as Maya's nerves. "I'm not scared," Maya said.

"I didn't ask you if you were scared," Billie said. "I asked you what you hear."

"I hear peril . . . and uncertainty. It sounds like a forest full of threat, Billie. Don't do it," Maya said hastily, her back against the side fence inside their little schoolyard pen and her eyes fixed on Darkwood Forest beyond the back fence.

Billie said, "Thank you for your assistance, Maya," and trotted back to where her last victim, Ovid, was waiting. "Ovid, you're the shortest of us all, are you not? What do you see under the fence? What are the rumblings you feel so close to the ground?"

"Actually, I'm taller than you, Billie."

"That's beside the point. When you look behind me, what do you feel in your heart?"

"I feel like the unknown is singing to me. It's like a Siren calling to me to risk it all," Ovid said, as Billie moved closer to him with a fierce look in her eye. He'd never seen this side of Billie, so he too started backing away from her. "I know I shouldn't follow the voice. I know you shouldn't follow that voice either. All of us know you shouldn't follow that voice, but you're going to anyway, aren't you, Billie?"

"I'm just an ordinary goat, just like you, Ovid. Like all of you,

I have four legs, two horns, two eyes, and one mouth, but something makes me different. Something makes me special. What is it?" Billie asked the audience as she backed Ovid up until he was next to Virgil and Maya. The three of them were pushed back up against the fence all in a row, shortest to tallest: little Ovid, then medium Maya, and finally, the tallest of them, Virgil. "Get up. All of you. Let me hear your hooves." Billie started tapping her hoof rhythmically in the dirt. Soon they were all tapping in unison with her. She stopped her own tapping, then quickly trotted straight toward the back fence that separated her and her mates from Darkwood Forest. She stopped in front of the fence and stared at the shadowy trees long enough to let her fears escape from her mind.

Kate bleated to her, "Billie, come back!"

Maya and her friends chimed in too. "Billie, come on. Come back!"

All of the kids broke their silence and cried, "Come back, Billie!"

Without turning, Billie slowly walked backward and counted her steps. She knew every step would be important for getting herself over the back fence. Once she was behind all the kids, she stopped and yelled, "Start the countdown!"

Homer, the one that had dared her in the first place, spoke up. "How're you gonna clear that fence? You can't jump that high. None of us can."

"You may not be able to, but I can. Just start the countdown."

"You're going to fail." Homer looked at her in disbelief.

"Just look at Darkwood Forest and start the countdown. Don't be scared. I'll be back in the stable faster than Caesar can polish off a bowl of breakfast kibble."

Ovid started counting. "Ten, nine, eight . . ."

The does joined in. "Seven, six . . ."

Then Virgil added his voice. "Five, four . . ."

Finally, Homer gave up and joined in with the excitement of the stunt. "THREE, TWO, ONE!"

Before the group had gotten to "one," Billie had galloped full force toward Ovid, Maya, and Virgil. She hopped onto Ovid's back first, then Maya's, and then finally Virgil's, the tallest kid. All three goats were lined up against the fence. Billie paused briefly on Virgil's back and gathered her balance. She thought the top of the fence was just beyond her reach, but then she remembered that Antoni had already leapt this distance effortlessly before, so she decided to make a go of it anyway. She was in midair, and her big plan to leap to the top of the fence from her friend's back was not looking good.

Billie stuck a hoof out as gravity pulled her back toward the earth inside the pen. Her hoof caught the top rail of the fence and stopped her from falling.

"She's gonna fall!" Maya said in panic for her friend.

"No, she's not," Ovid said from the bottom of the staircase Billie had just formed out of her friends. "She'll figure it out. She always does."

Billie had gotten a second and a third hoof onto the top rail now, then a fourth. She took a deep breath to compose herself, then stood up straight on top of the rail, balanced and ready.

"You did it!" Kate cried out.

"Not yet I haven't. I still have a beautiful round rock to retrieve. I have to go in there, pick one up, *and* make it back in one piece to prove my worth." Billie took her first step along the top beam. On the edge of their hooves, her audience watched each and every step she took. Ovid ran around the others that were in his way and followed her every step on the way to the back fence.

In his usual way, Ovid injected random thoughts about the origin of her stunt. "You know," he said, "the first fence that ever came to be, Billie . . . it was really just a wall. It was made of giant stacked rocks."

"Not now, Ovid. I'm almost there." Billie focused on her balance, and as she got close to the back fence, she asked him, "Are you sure you want to be this close to Darkwood?"

"Billie, I'd follow you anywhere if you'd just listen."

"Listen to what, Ovid?"

"Me," Ovid replied.

"I always listen, but I can't say I always obey!" Billie said.

"Don't do it, Billie. It's not worth it," Ovid pleaded with his best friend.

"Worth is always subjective when it's said, isn't it?" Billie pondered the words of her closest friend for a moment. Their eyes were locked while she was still atop the fence, then she said what she needed to say as simply as she could possibly put it: "Bye!"

Chapter 7

"**B**ILLLLIEEEEE! BILLLLLLLIEEEEEE!" Ovid continually bleated for his friend, but she was nowhere to be seen. She didn't say a thing to him after she landed on the other side of the fence. The last thing he heard was "Bye," and then she made her way up the piney slope. When Billie got to the first little peak, she went over it and disappeared without a word.

Virgil trotted up to his friend. "Time shall make all things well, Ovid. Let us depart from the fence. Our own well-being cannot be improved by peering into such an evil region."

"BILLLLIEEEEE!" Ovid tried again hopelessly.

Antoni had been napping inside the barn. After hearing all the racket, she calmly strutted out of a narrow gap in the barn siding and jumped on top of a fence post between Darkwood and Ovid. She looked down at the little buckling. "What's this fuss all about?"

"Billie vaulted herself beyond our barricade and vanished without so much as a word," Virgil said.

"She'll be fine," Antoni replied.

"What do you mean, she'll be fine?" Ovid was suddenly in a panic.

"She'll be fine. You'll see." Antoni jumped down and disappeared into a tunnel weaved into the grasses.

"Oh, Billie! Billie, darling! I'm back now! Where are you!?" Ovid could hear Billie's mother calling. The grownup goats were beginning to return to the farmyard in small groups, and Billie was still nowhere to be seen. "Billie! Where are you, love?" Edna tried again. "Ovid? Are you over there? Where's my Billie?"

"Yes, ma'am," he said sheepishly. "She . . . left."

"Left? What do you mean she left? There's nowhere to go," Edna said.

"She did a little stunt, but she'll be right back."

"What kind of stunt?!"

"Don't tell her!" Maya whispered too loudly to Ovid.

"Don't tell her what?" Edna asked as she turned to Ovid. "Come out with it, Ovid. I am her mother!"

"She . . . she hopped the back fence and went into Darkwood Forest." Ovid spilled the cud. He thought his guilt would subside if the truth came out, but it didn't.

Edna panicked and trotted around, aimlessly calling for her daughter. As the last of the goats came down the hill, Caesar was following just behind them. He saw how panicked Billie's mother was and ran straight up to her. "What's happening, doe?" he shrieked. "Where's Billie?"

"I don't know. I don't know. I don't know," she repeated dolefully, staring toward Darkwood with a blank expression.

Doctor Sylvia could see Edna was too shaken to give Caesar the news, so she spoke for her. "Ovid has just informed us that Billie hopped the back fence. She's in Darkwood Forest now, and no one has seen her for several minutes. What can we do, Caesar?"

"She needs to listen to me when I tell her not to do something.

All I do is look out for you goats, and this is how you repay me?" Caesar blurted out his frustration.

"Can't you go get her?" Sappho asked the herd dog.

Caesar looked off into nowhere. He had the look of a leader who was undecided, lost, and anchored by fear. After a long while, he made a decision. "I'll have to get the farmer."

Chapter 8

For the first time in her entire life, Billie was alone. Her heartbeat felt so loud inside of her that she was certain it echoed throughout the forest. Every new noise made her whip her head around to see what it was, but she never spotted anything. She couldn't spot a single animal, though she could hear the woods absolutely teeming with life. Insects and birds made most of the noise, but she could hear a stream off in the distance too. Overhead, the branches clapped together. It seemed as if the trees were greeting one another by shaking leaves. Everything talked with everything else that lived there, but she couldn't understand a word of it. She wasn't part of this place—she was just in it.

The longer she was in there, the safer she began to feel. The safer she felt, the braver her steps grew. Soon enough, her steps hastened and brought her to the edge of a small gully. At the bottom of this modest ravine, she could see the noisy little stream that she had been hearing as it twisted its way through beautiful rocks of various sizes. Some of them were exactly the sort of smooth and rounded stone that she wanted to bring back.

"Perfect!" Billie shrieked and immediately knew she'd been too loud. The chatty forest all around her stopped talking for a moment, and she became keenly aware of her own presence in these woods. Looking back and forth, she saw that there weren't any good hiding places, so she went down into the stream's little gully as quickly and quietly as she could. As she entered the stream, the cold water flowed over her hooves. She looked around. From this vantage point, all she could see was the edge of the stream's high, sloped banks and the tall trees that tried to block the sky. She took big breaths, hoping to calm her spooked nerves.

When she saw that the coast was clear, she was able to explore her surroundings and look for the stone she needed, right between her hooves. She noticed the sensation of moving water on her wet legs for the first time. It felt soothing to her. She noticed the variety of boulders around her. Some were huge. Those were all rough. They looked powerful and immovable, but surely each of them had moved at least once before. Surely they could not have been born where they were now. They must have seen other places before this one.

Billie noticed the little rocks that were submerged in the fast-moving water and ones that weren't. The ones in the moving water seemed to have smoother surfaces than the ones that hadn't seen adventurous waters yet. The farther the rocks were from the action, the more jagged and rigid they seemed to be. She stepped forward and into a patch of tiny pebbles that were so small that they looked as if they'd soon become sand. And there, stuck in actual sand, she saw a beautiful, well-rounded rock. The creek must have dried up around it recently because the water was no longer touching it. It was smooth like the ones in the fast-moving water. The one she picked out was brown, with black lines running through it and little white spots here and there. It reminded her of her mother and her grandmother because their fur had a combination of the same sort of black, brown, and white. So, this little stone must have reminded her of herself too, because she looked just like her mother and her grandmother.

"Here! Here!" a raven called out.

Billie looked up to see where the voice was coming from. "Shhhh!" she whispered forcefully. "You're gonna give me away, bird."

"Here! Here!" The bird ignored her plea. "Here! Here!" The raven looked at her with no sympathy. "You'll be fine. Symbiosis. You'll be fine. Stay here. Here! Here!"

Billie finally spotted the raven above her head on a low pine branch, and then something else caught her eye: a dark, ominous tail.

"Here! Here!" The raven wasn't giving up and was gaining confidence every second on its branch.

Feathers suddenly flew into the air as a black-and-gray ball of fury sprang into action. It was so fast it was practically a blur to Billie. Her every muscle tensed, readying for flight, but she wasn't sure if this second predator had noticed her. She could bolt if anything changed in the slightest.

"Get back here, you chicken! You're not the only symbiotic thing in the forest, you instigator!" Antoni yelled out at the crow. She then turned and smirked slyly at her farmyard friend as the crow flew off. "Maybe next time?" she asked quietly, winking at Billie.

"My heart was in my throat," Billie said to Antoni. The panic she was feeling had yet to subside entirely.

"You're fiiiiiiine." The cat drew out the word lazily, hoping to calm Billie down. "You're just at the edge of the woods, kid. If you get deep in there, that's where the real danger starts."

"Sappho's story . . . I thought I was the hare," Billie said as her lungs tried to catch their breath.

"It's just a story, my toeless friend." Antoni made her way

down the tree and onto solid ground. She continued moving toward Billie, staring her in the eye. "Wait, which story did Sappho tell you?"

"'The Wolf and the Hare.'"

"Ah, that's a good one." Antoni thought about how Sappho's tale might have impacted Billie but decided to let her say what that impact was. "In your own words, what's the point of the story?"

"Not to go in the woods?" Billie answered.

Antoni jumped onto her friend's back. "That's only part of it. The story says not to meddle in the affairs of wolves, for they're quite smart, and you're quite tasty." She waited for Billie to laugh, but maybe her joke didn't land. "To them, not me. Really, though, if you're gonna be out here, just be smart. If one wolf sees you, make sure they never see you again. Run, hide, climb, do whatever you have to, but always have an exit strategy."

"What's an exit strategy?" Billie asked.

Antoni answered, "It's a way to escape safely when something unexpected happens. I'm guessing you didn't have one of those, did you?" The feline jumped down off Billie's back and climbed out of the little gully.

"No, not exactly," Billie said as she looked up toward the cat now perched on the boulder above her.

"Don't worry about it, kid. Just make sure you have one next time you leave the farm." Antoni tried to find some common ground. "Goats have nine lives like cats, right?"

"I think we just get the one," Billie said.

"Ah, then you'll just have to be a bit more cautious than I am. But not too cautious! You'll never do anything in life if you're too cautious. But still . . . you can't always trust your surroundings, so there's no substitute for double-checking, sister. Have a plan. Look twice before you leap, you know? Listen to the signs, 'cause they're definitely out there. Know what I'm saying?"

"What kinds of signs?" Billie asked.

"You gotta listen to everything. Everything in this world talks, even if you haven't learned the language. Did you hear the insects quiet down?"

"No."

"By getting quiet, the insects told me a bird was nearby. I had that raven spotted before it even landed on the branch. The raven spotted you a few seconds later. That's how I almost got to him. You distracted him for me. Otherwise, he probably would've heard me sooner. You see, everything in here is looking for an easy meal, and everything in here is hunted by something else. Everything but the wolves. They rule at the top, but that doesn't mean there isn't plenty of room underneath them in this grand pyramid of life, so don't let the pecking order stop you from enjoying your journey." Antoni finished her sentence, then jumped onto Billie's back again.

"What's a pyramid?" Billie asked.

"It's like a stack of stones. One stone is on top, a bunch of stones are on the bottom, and there's a bunch in between."

"Where are you, then?" Billie turned her head to look at the companion on her back as she asked the question.

"Well, right on top of you." Antoni smirked with her eyes.

Billie clarified. "No, I mean where are you on this stack of animals out here?"

"I don't know. Somewhere up above that bird, that's for sure. That doesn't matter, though—you have to study all forms of life if you want to understand the language of the woodlands. But quit wasting time, little sister. We need to get back home. *Mush!*"

Billie started her ascent out of the little mountain stream but stopped in her tracks. "Would you have killed that raven if you could have?"

"Nah, most prey isn't worth the risk. If it knocked me off that branch, there goes another life, and I'm down to eight. Catching that bird wasn't worth one of my nine lives, but you can bet it was worth one of yours, seeing it's your one and only. I just read the situation and reacted. Sometimes that's what it's all about. You see, killing that bird wasn't going to help you, but chasing it off might have saved your hide because it was calling for something with big teeth to turn you into a carcass so it could eat the leftovers. That's the symbiosis it was talking about."

"Either way, thanks, Antoni."

"Hey, that little rock down there kinda suits you! It's the one you were kicking around just before that stupid bird started messing with you, isn't it?" Antoni chirped.

"How did you—"

"My eyes and ears are always on notice. I've also been in here longer than you knew," Antoni said.

Remembering the dare, Billie grasped the little brown stone with white spots and black lines running through it between her teeth. She stowed it away behind her lips and started her return journey to the farm. "Anks!" Billie said with her mouth full.

Chapter 9

Edna stared hopelessly into Darkwood Forest while the rest of the farm shuffled about in panic. Every goat was bleating for Billie. They all wanted her to come home. Caesar barked appeals at the front door of the farmer's house until his relentlessness gained the farmer's attention. No one was behaving like themselves. Not their ordinary selves, at least.

"It's my fault, Miss Edna," Ovid cried to Billie's mother. "I shouldn't have fallen for her trick. I didn't know what she was gonna do. She lined us up and used us like stairs to get away." Edna was still in her own world of panic and didn't even turn to the little buckling talking to her.

By the back fence near Darkwood, Virgil paced back and forth, periodically bleating his friend's name. He swung his head back and forth on his elongated neck as he looked for any sign of Billie over the top of the fence. In all the time that passed, there hadn't been a single sign of hope, and it was getting dark.

But then, there was something off in the distance. "Billie?" Virgil asked himself, then narrowed his eyes for confirmation. "Billie!" he cried, looking around, but no one else seemed to hear the message he was sharing amid all the bleating and calling, so he cried out even louder. "She's back! She's back! Billie's back!"

Edna broke her silence. "Where?" she shouted.

"She's right there! She has that cat on her back! She's right there!"

Billie was calmly walking in a zigzag pattern down the slope where she was last seen by Ovid, but this time around with Antoni in tow. The farmer had just come out of the house at Caesar's noisy request and saw all the commotion. At first, Caesar ambled toward the doeling-feline pair, then broke into a full rotary gallop.

"You need to get your act together right now, Billie Someday! I told you to never go into Darkwood Forest, and what did you do? What part of 'never' did you not understand?!" Antoni was shaken out of her dazed slumber by Caesar's berating of Billie. She immediately darted off. In no time flat, the gray Maine coon was out of sight. "Get back in the pen right now, Billie Someday! You will never be out of my sight ever again, you impossible creature! Go! Go! Go!"

The farmer caught up to them and quickly scooped Billie up into his soft arms. Caesar was still barking orders: "Tell her! Tell her! She's not supposed to leave! She only goes where we tell her, right?" The farmer kindly snapped his fingers at the dog, and the canine's rant ended immediately.

Billie was safely escorted back toward the schoolyard pen in the farmer's arms, pressed against the red wool sweater he wore every day, and Edna chased alongside them. The farmer saw now that the schoolyard gate had been opened, so he took his knit hat off, scratched his messy head of hair, walked over, and closed it. He started to lower Billie back into her pen and changed his mind. Instead, he walked around from the schoolyard barn over toward the higher fence of the grownup pen and put Billie down in there.

All her life, Billie had wondered what the grownup goat pen

would look like, but after the farmer put her down, all she could see were sets of doe legs. She was surrounded by just about every pair of them, minus her own mama's legs. The does' reactions to the farmer showed they adored him, and he must have loved them too. He just stood there and kept reaching into the pockets of his overalls and petting each one of them until they were satisfied.

"Treat?" Ovid's mother asked with a short bleat.

"Treat?" asked another mother.

"Treat" was repeated by most of the grownups until the farmer gave each mother a sugar cube. They all chewed their little delicacies one by one and walked away satisfied. As the adults trotted off, Billie's view slowly became unobstructed. Through a clearing in the goat legs, she saw the biggest creature she'd ever seen looking right back at her. She was certain it was the bear Ovid talked about, so she crept backward along the fence, looking for something that might resemble an exit strategy.

The familiar voice of Caesar came from the other side of the fence. "Look out, mate. That cow might eat ya. Ha!"

"Mooooo!" The cow might have welcomed the neophyte with her "moo," but Billie couldn't understand what she said. The farmer walked over to the cow and grabbed her bridle. He led her into a separate fenced area and started filling her water barrel. All the mother goats were watching this commotion with common interest.

"Oh no," Ovid's mama said, as she watched the farmer make a beeline for the grownup water trough. He got down on a knee and toggled something at the bottom of the vessel. Water puddled up and slowly disappeared into the soil. Then he walked straight toward a water pail and kicked it over. Next, he pushed over the water barrel, then the trough next to it, and walked out of the gate, disappearing from view. Billie walked over to the gate to try to see what he was doing but couldn't spot him. Billie thought he must have gone over to her friends in the schoolyard pen.

"No more water for us grownup goats. I guess it's time you kids start fending for yourselves. Apparently, you're being weaned." Ovid's mother looked down at her son's friend with a sympathetic eye.

The farmer showed back up and opened the gate to the grownup pen. Ovid's mother started to walk over to where her sons were entering through their gate, and the farmer shooed her back into the grownup pen. Maya came trotting in, followed by her two friends, then Kate. Next came Virgil, and last, Ovid.

"Hello, Billie," Kate said with a wink. "I knew you'd make it."

"Billie! You're back!" Ovid said happily.

Trailing behind all the other kids was Homer. Billie had never noticed how fast he was growing before, but she could see his muscles rippling along his chest and shoulders as he trotted. None of the other goats looked quite like that when they moved. Billie thought he looked handsome as he trotted right up to her and stopped.

"Welcome back! It looks like you just got us kicked out of the schoolyard pen, Billie," Homer said with a grin on his face. "What do you have to say for yourself?"

Billie didn't say a thing; she just grinned back at him.

"You gotta say *something*, Billie!" Ovid said.

Billie spit out the little brown stone with the white spots and black lines running through it. It landed near Homer's hoof—he looked down at it, lifted his head, and looked Billie in the eye. Billie looked Homer right back in his. "Did it," she told him. "And just in case you've forgotten which goat you dared, I'm Billie Someday, the greatest of all time. Nice to meet you, kid."

Chapter 10

"**N**o way!" Homer exclaimed. He was impressed.

Edna abruptly pushed through the welcoming party. "Do you have some kind of death wish, young lady?"

"No, Mama. I just have a thirst for—" Billie tried to answer.

"A thirst for dying while I'm here all alone? While I'm scared to death?"

"Mama, I have a thirst for life. I'm just being myself."

"You need to be yourself, right here on this farm! Not out there! The world is too big and too dangerous for you to be running off all alone!" Edna scolded.

"What's that?" Billie said, looking past her mother with wide eyes.

"It's just a cow. Now look at me and focus on what I'm trying to tell you because I love you and want what's—"

"The cow's over there, Mama." Billie motioned toward the cow, then back at the awe-inspiring object. "What's *that*?"

Edna turned to see what her daughter was seeing. Nothing was out of the ordinary, in her opinion, but she had seen the object of Billie's curiosity countless times. "What are you talking about?"

"Look up that hill."

"Okay."

"Do you see that thing that's behind it? That's the biggest thing I've ever seen."

"The Matterhorn?" Edna turned to face her daughter, already knowing what she must be thinking. "We don't ever go up there. I won't let it hurt you, because you're never going near it. All we do is go up the hill, graze, and come back. That's it. We never go near the peak, much less the base of it, so you don't have to worry about it."

Billie remembered the tiny little pebbles she had seen in the little mountain stream. She thought that if she herself were the size of a pebble, then the Matterhorn would still be bigger than the barn. Way bigger. This Matterhorn was unfathomably big to her.

"What . . . is a Matterhorn?" Billie asked with confusion in her voice.

"Nothing's a Matterhorn," her mother replied quickly.

"It's a mountain, sweetheart," Sappho said to her granddaughter as she approached. "And I believe it's impromptu story time. Right, Edna?"

The little safe world that all eight kids knew had just gotten abruptly swept into a world far bigger than they'd ever be able to fully understand. The schoolyard stable that was on one side, the farmer's log cabin that was on the other, Big Tractor Road out front, and Darkwood Forest behind them were no longer their only world. Now the giant Darkwood Forest that loomed over them was a part of this new world, as was the Matterhorn.

Their lives had just gone from being the inside of a box to being a place that appeared unconfined. And it *would* be unconfined if it weren't for the fences. The new fences around the grownup pen defined new boundaries for them, and the new boundaries were the first of the new rules that would now be applied to them. And now it was time for these eight kids to learn some harsh truths and new rules about their way of life here on the farm.

Chapter 11

Clonk . . . cliiing . . . clink-clink-clink.

Sappho knocked a water pail over so she could tap its bottom with her hoof and gain the attention of the herd. "It's time, everyone, it's time. Everyone to Story Tree Hill. If you're in the presentation, it's time—prepare your parts."

Billie looked around, and there was only one tree inside this new pen, so there was no confusion about where to go. The tree didn't have a single leaf on it, but it still looked alive enough to sprout fresh leaves in the spring. The tree was up on a mound, and with the mound aiding the height of the tree, together they rose above everything on the farm, even the barn. The tree and hill were directly in the center of this arena, making them a natural beacon for its inhabitants. There was also a boulder on the hill that sat at the base of the tree. It looked a bit like one of the large boulders Billie had seen by the creek in Darkwood, and it was big enough to hold several goats at the same time, if need be. Billie was unsure of what this tree and hill meant to the goats, but it certainly looked important to her. Far more important than the stacked tires by the little red dirt mound in the schoolyard.

The farmer looked across the pen. Seeing that the chaos accompanying Billie's escape had passed, he headed back to the farmhouse, followed by Caesar. Just as he reached the door, he snapped his fingers at Caesar, and the herd dog's head dropped in disappointment. He knew he wasn't to be invited inside today. "Awwww crikey," he groaned from over on the farmer's porch, letting his front legs slide outward and his hind legs collapse.

"Cheer up, Caesar. It could be worse. Any other day he might have kicked you off the farm for letting the golden milk-kid escape," Antoni said pointedly as she headed toward Story Tree Hill to watch the production.

"There's nothing golden about that kid, and you know it," Caesar replied.

"Whatever you say, my most sacred chieftain of fenced-in soil, Holy Roman Emperor Canineous Caesar, first of his name, protector of this farm realm, ruler to all beasts of burden . . . and the dog who's never tasted the golden dairy product," Antoni said. She knew Caesar had never sampled the prized milk that Billie's breed could eventually produce. Antoni, on the other hand, was very familiar with it, having tasted Edna's and Sappho's milk many times.

"Grrrrrrr," Caesar growled humorlessly.

A few moments later, Antoni walked up to join the goats around Story Tree Hill. She parked herself right next to Billie just as the members of the presentation were beginning to take their places. Billie watched wide-eyed as the elders climbed to background positions up on the hill.

The adults placed the eight kids in the best location to follow the production. Looking up the hill, Billie watched Doctor Sylvia take a background position with the other elders while her grandmother, Sappho, took center stage.

Billie looked around for her mother in the audience. She was nowhere to be seen, and the thoughts of her mother's whereabouts preoccupied her so much that she didn't even notice the production beginning until Virgil nudged her into paying attention.

Sappho began the presentation with the support of the elders behind her. "*You* and *I* must eat *food* to live," she began. "We all know this to be true, but what you don't know is that *food* can bring us to our enemies. It's a dangerous world out there for us, but if we abide by the rules that govern who we are, we can diminish the risks that our herd lives with as farm goats."

"Long ago," she resumed, "our ancestors lived in an environment with risks, risks that far exceeded those we deal with now. This is because they lived in the mountains, and the mountains have always been steep . . . and wild."

Sappho repositioned and gathered herself for this all-important part of her speech. It would lay the foundation for why they lived inside the fences with the farmer instead of freely in the wild. "Mountain life forced our ancestors to find ways to survive amid constant danger. Each step on a narrow path to find food might just be the last, and catching up with an old friend often required leaps that could end disastrously. Each time food became scarce, the herd would descend from the highlands and head for greener pastures below, but they were chased back up the mountains by predators. Most often those predators were wolves." Sappho stared at Billie to make sure she was listening. "It was a dangerous lifestyle with limited food and water, and nothing but uncomfortable resting places exist in the highlands. This made even something as simple as peaceful sleep a scarce resource. The result of these combined hardships forced herds to maintain modest sizes."

Sappho gazed across at the huge herd she was so proud to be a part of. "And this is the beginning of our story, our livelihood, the reason for our ways as farm goats. More and more often, the winters our ancestors lived through in the highlands would cause them to run out of nutrition. So, more and more often they would decide to leave the security of the mountains and steer themselves into the realm of the wolves below. They did so knowing they would likely be chased. Traveling below was risky, but they also needed food to live."

Sappho locked eyes with several of the other kids in her captivated audience, letting the idea of their ancestors' risks sink in. "One year, it got worse. The winter was so long and harsh that the mountain goats were forced to make another decision to venture down the mountain. But this time, the winter was so harsh and the snow was so deep that enough food couldn't be found even in Darkwood. Our ancestors had to journey across its borders, all the way over to our grazing hill, in order to find the food they needed to survive. The very same hill that is able to feed us all year long."

Sappho began to speak more loudly. "Now, we know Darkwood can provide cover for the small and sleek, but we are neither small nor sleek, and neither were our ancestors. So making it across Darkwood's borders, unscathed, would require luck for the mountain goats, but this particular winter that I speak of was not a lucky winter." She looked up, imagining their struggle, then picked up where she left off. "The unlivable conditions that winter forced our ancestors to make a very difficult journey to cross Darkwood. One that proved even more difficult once the wolves began to attack."

"After losing a few of its members to these attacks during the crossing, the mountain goats pulled into a tight circle. The large does and bucks stayed on the outside, and the kids were kept in the middle. The wolves kept a safe distance, knowing the great racks of the bucks and rigid horns of the does made formidable barriers. Our ancestors were huddled together safely for the time being, but the wolves knew that eventually the mountain goats would need food and water. They knew that if the mountain goats moved to find food and water, the circle would surely break, making it vulnerable. The mountain goats needed a solution."

Sappho turned around and faced the elders but continued her monologue. "Two solutions arose—spread out, run and hide until spring . . . or head for the bright fire that they could see down in the valley. The wolves feared fire, especially ones created by man, and this fire in the valley belonged to men."

Billie felt the sadness in her grandmother's voice hearing those words, even without seeing her face when she delivered them.

"Our ancestors knew that, long ago, man had harnessed certain wolves for their hunting skills and for their ability to protect, shaping them into the dogs we see today, like Caesar. Dog obeyed mankind in exchange for a place by the fire, a place that had regular meals and was safe. These wolves had chosen to become dogs. Goats had the same chance to unite with man now, but if they did, they would be changed forever. The biggest and strongest mountain goats wanted to keep running in the old way, while the docile ones preferred to test the will of man."

Sappho turned to the crowd below her. "The goats choosing domestication chose wisely. Adaptation to farm-style lives required that certain changes to their bodies would become part of life. Like the dog, we too had to obey man, and mankind used our many gifts for their own. Using our offerings, man no longer needed to hunt or gather. With goats, man could stay in one place, build, cultivate, and thrive. Men became farmers like our farmer. And farm life is safer for mankind, for dogs, and for large goat herds."

Sappho glanced down, then back up, and her voice softened. "Man traveled to suit our nutritional needs, and dogs kept us safe at night when man was asleep. The longer we stayed with man, the more we changed. We became smaller, our horns shrunk, and we needed to be milked more often. Even if we had wanted to return to our prior homes on the mountain, we couldn't. We had to be protected and milked. We had changed. While our ancestors are still mountain goats, the very ibex that grace the highlands today, we are now farm goats down in the valley. There is a difference between ibex and farm goats that we must accept. Farm goats work with farmers to make a good life. Mountain goats exist in chaos. What we have is a far safer existence."

An elder from behind spoke loudly. "With security comes sacrifice."

Sappho was expecting to hear her fellow elder's words. "Yes, and some sacrifices are easier than others. It's not so hard to provide our surplus of milk for the farmer to use and to allow the farmer and his dog to make decisions for us. But what is difficult is what our lifestyle does to our bucks and bucklings."

Ovid, Virgil, and Homer all perked up when they heard this message that targeted them. Their hearts raced in anticipation of the next message they would hear. The mother goats began to bleat their emotions: "Whyhahahy?!"

"No-oohohohoohhh!"

The crowd continued to murmur until it got quiet enough for Sappho to finish. She made no eye contact during any part of this speech, knowing the pain it is for mothers to let go of a loved one. "Most of our bucklings must leave the farm eventually. Bucks must move away to spread to our greater family on other farms. We must spread out our herd to survive, and they must be passed from farm to farm. Some bucklings might stay here and become wethers, but, regardless, great sacrifice is made by all bucks, and almost all mothers must eventually say goodbye to our male heirs."

"What's a *wether*?" Ovid asked nervously.

"I'll tell you later, kid," Antoni said to him with kindness in her voice.

Billie felt uncomfortable with this whole idea and looked around for her mother once again, but Edna was nowhere to be seen. Billie was surrounded by her friends and everyone else's mothers, but she felt alone dealing with this shocking news without her own. What was this strange world she had just been introduced to? None of it made sense, and why wasn't her mother here for her?

First the top of Edna's head appeared, then her eyes peeked over the top of the boulder, and she continued climbing up until she was atop it. She was glowing with the sun behind her, but she seemed nervous about something. With all this talk of sacrifice, Billie felt her stomach drop. She was nervous that her mother would be sacrificed for the farmer right there on this very rock.

"Milk." Edna's voice was trembling. "At the center of all we do for the farmer is our milk. If we can provide milk, we can stay on the farm. All does and doelings can stay together here if we do. I am the youngest mother in the herd, so it is my duty to explain what you must go through to make milk of your own."

Edna looked around at each of the elders. "Each of us is like a flower, and you doelings are, too. You are like a seed, and a seed grows until it becomes a flower, then blossoms. You haven't yet blossomed, but when you do, you will have kids of your own. You will provide milk to nourish them, as well as to nourish the farmer, and this is how our circle of life will continue. Having children gives us the ability to make milk. It is our duty for you and for each other to have kids. So when you blossom . . ." A lump in her throat slowed her delivery. "So when you blossom, it will be your time to . . . pollinate."

Billie was relieved to know that her mother was only speaking of sacrifices, but her awkward speech didn't hit any marks. *This is weird*, Billie thought.

"To pollinate, we must spend quality time with the buck that the farmer arranges for us. And so we must accept the arranged buck on to our farm and be kind hosts to them while they're here. We must make them comfortable . . . just as we like to be comfortable." Edna backed herself down from the top of the boulder and walked down the hill toward the kids. "Follow me. It's time you kids met our guest buck, Dante."

Chapter 12

Edna led the kids around to the backside of the hill and toward the back fence. They followed her in a single file line, and when they got to the back fence, they lined up along it and peered out across an empty pen over to the next mysterious one. The next pen was dark, had tall wooden fencing surrounding it, and was so well fortified that you could hardly see anything inside but a few cracks where some light peeked through. Surely nothing on four hooves that got trapped in that kind of fence would ever be able to break free from it on its own.

"You smell like runts," a deep voice barked at them, but the kids couldn't see anything. The voice boomed from everywhere and nowhere. Then they heard a breath exhale from somewhere out in front of them. It was enormous and frightening. Little Kate backed up, turned, and shifted her weight so she could make a break away from it, but Edna stopped her. They still hadn't spotted the goat that went by the name Dante, but a cloud of hot air dispersed over the top of the tall wooden fence that they could all see.

"You'll be fine. He's not going to hurt you. He can't. And besides, he's a kind buck. I promise. Give him a chance, Kate," Edna said.

Ovid turned his head when he saw a tuft of weeds rustle through the cracks. "There!" he shouted. "There he is!"

"Where?" Billie asked.

"He's in the next pen over!" he shouted.

Billie looked beyond the neighboring pen to the next pen over. All she saw was the towering fort. It was ultimately still a fence, but it was so much higher than their schoolyard one. Taller than the grownup pen's fence, too. It was almost as tall as the farmer, maybe taller. Billie finally made some sense of what Edna was trying to show them, and looking through the cracks, she could make out the rough outline of a black-and-brown mess of long hair maneuvering inside the barrier.

The voice boomed again. "Get out of here, rascals. Not one of you cares one iota about old Dante. Remove your carcasses! There's nothing to see here. I'm not some attraction brought here to ogle over. I'm a buck. Treat me like one, for heaven's sake!"

WHAM! Dante crashed into the fence with the enormous force of his gigantic horns.

"It's fine, kids—just stay where you are. He's frustrated. It's not about you," Edna said.

"It's about the runts, and you know it, doe. My home was taken from me, and they dragged me down through the seven circles of hellfire to appease the milk-makers. I've had enough! I just want my home back! I'm a buck! Treat me like one, for goat's sake!" Dante's words sounded darker with each new sentence.

WHAM! Dante kicked the fence with all the force he could muster up.

"Dante, you're going to be fine. You're our guest at our little farm now, and all of us are your friends. You're going to be happy here. You won't want to leave—you'll see," Edna continued to coax him.

"You take me away from my own farm, my own family, and for what? So you can force me from one fenced island to the next and the next? They burned my farm and destroyed my memories. Why?" Dante's voice went from furious to hopeless.

"Why did they burn your farm?" Billie asked innocently. "Your farm is your home, and your home is their home as well, isn't it?"

"What is your name, little one?" Dante asked calmly.

"Billie Someday . . ." She hesitated and then continued, ". . . the greatest of all time."

Billie had no idea what had come over her. Normally she was calling herself the greatest because of her stunts, but this time it felt as if it was her name. She had just introduced herself by it, after all, and she said it as though she believed it, because she *did* believe it. She was Billie Someday, the greatest of all time, and *knew* it for the first time.

"Well, Billie Someday, if you want to be the greatest, you've got to beat the greatest," Dante said sharply. "And the greatest isn't sitting in your pen. You haven't faced the greatest of us. The greatest is bigger, stronger, faster, and smarter than any you know."

"My grandma is pretty smart, and I am too," Billie said defiantly.

"So is your mother, Billie, and trust me," Edna said sternly, "you don't need to go hoof to hoof with Dante. He's our friend."

"How do you plan on besting the greatest, runt? Are you going to push harder than any goat has ever pushed? Are you going to out-ram a pair of horns twice the size of your entire body? Are you going to face the big alpha or tuck your little tail in and scoot?" Dante went after Billie.

"It doesn't matter. I'm gonna be on top," Billie said.

"You don't even know what that means. The burden is something you don't ever wanna feel. There's a relentless expectation to perform magic, once you get there. Pick a better goal, Billie

Someday—being on top isn't a tenth of what it seems," he said sharply.

"You don't know—you've never been there," Billie said. "You've only been on fenced islands. You said it yourself."

"What are you talking about, kid?" he said. "Being at the top is lonely. That's what the fenced islands are about. You think I can share this burden? It is mine and mine alone. I get all the credit if the kids turn out well and all the blame if they don't. You won't ever know what that means."

"Well, I'm talking about the very top," Billie insisted. "It's a place you'll never go. I'm going to be the goat that gets there and the goat you can never be."

"And so what do you think this very top is, little doeling?" Dante asked.

"I'm gonna be a mountain-climbing goat, and I'm gonna climb to the top of the Matterhorn. The very top of everything!" she exclaimed.

The giant creature turned and looked through the slots of his pen and couldn't spot this bold little challenger. He paced back and forth, breathing in and out through his nostrils. The kids could all see the hot vapor coming from his nose with each breath. When he exhaled, clouds of hot air hung in the frosty air, then slowly disappeared into the northern winds. He stopped pacing and put his giant hooves on the wooden wall separating them. Billie saw his enormous twisting horns rising above the top of the fence, then she saw his sad golden eyes peer over the top as they gazed back and forth down the line of eight little kids. Any questions that Billie had about the size of Dante suddenly vanished like his breath did in the wind. He was huge.

"Which one of you is Billie Someday?" the great beast asked.

"I am," Billie said, her head held high.

Dante turned his neck sharply and focused on the little dwarf goat with fire and fury in her eyes. He locked eyes with her and stared her down. Suddenly his head tilted back, and he laughed heartily toward the sky. "Haw. Haw. Haw."

Billie no longer felt so good about her chances of becoming the greatest of all time.

The farmer eased the tension when he suddenly dragged an older goat protesting his own predicament toward Dante's pen. "Bahahahahah, I don't like this! You do this to me every time. I don't wanna go-ohohohohoh! Please, farmer, don't make me go in. At least let me walk in on my own," the goat said, as the farmer ignored all of his pleas, dragging him across the empty lot toward Dante's pen. The farmer seemed to have come out of nowhere with this new goat. None of the kids had any clue who the new goat was.

"Who's that?" Virgil asked.

Antoni had just jumped up onto Billie's back. "That's Omar . . . the wether. You'll like him. Everyone does. That's why he's here."

The farmer let go of Omar's horns and opened the gate to Dante's pen.

"Oh, fine. I'll do it, but only 'cause you asked so nicely," the wether said sarcastically to the farmer, then walked agreeably into Dante's pen.

Dante took his two hooves off the fence, stood on all fours, and stared down his new, physically unimpressive pen-mate.

"Hi there. I'm Omar, your wether. At your service, sir," Omar said nervously.

The fiery eyes of the alpha goat were locked in on Omar as the gate was closed. The farmer walked away without so much as a casual introduction. Omar was going to have to fend for himself in there.

A giant roar of excitement came out of the giant buck. "Oh, FANTASTIC! I've been in here all alone! I'm so glad to meet you, Omar! You need any water? Something to eat?"

"Sure!" Omar replied confidently. The mood swung immediately in a favorable direction for all.

"Just a second, Omar. I need to tell my friend something," Dante said to his new pen-mate, then he jumped up on the fence again and peered down at Billie.

"Hey, kid, sorry I was grumpy. You're gonna do great! If you want to be the greatest of all time, be the greatest. Come on by if you ever wanna chat!" He tossed back his horns. "Ha! I just realized what that spells. I'll be cheering for you, kid! Get to the top! It'll be fantastic up there if you're good enough, and I'm sure you will be!" His sentences veered off as he cheerfully went back to the confines of his pen to hang out with his new fair-wether friend.

You see, most goats don't like being alone, and Dante was no exception. He had been all alone up until Omar showed up. Antoni couldn't have been more correct. Everyone loved Omar. Even a grumpy old lonely goat like Dante cheered up instantly in his presence.

Chapter 13

The next day began to break on their homestead, and a frosty mist hung in the air just above a lineation of sleeping heads. Maya was lying next to her mother, and they were both sleeping soundly, interlocked. Maya's friends were forming a sleeping line off of her, and Kate was resting her head on one of them. Ovid leaned on Kate, Virgil on Ovid, Homer on Virgil, and Edna was lying next to Homer, forming the caboose for the sleeping train of young goats out in the cool night air. Nine goats in all, with the two mothers on either end and only one kid missing.

The night prior, the elders told the kids all about the grazing hill and how they'd go see it first thing in the morning. When Billie heard about this hill, she just couldn't wait for morning. Slipping away from the sleeping pile sometime during the night, she got as close to the trail leading to the grazing hill as she possibly could and ignored the natural fear that most goats have of being alone. By being there, she was as close as she'd ever been to a shot at climbing this hill she'd heard about the day before. If she could get to the grazing hill they had described, she wondered how much closer she'd be to the Matterhorn.

Back over in the middle of the sleeping train, Maya's stomach growled with hunger, and it woke her up before the others. She got up and stretched her legs. Her balance was a little off, so she wobbled backward a bit, then forward some, and then side to side until she found her balance. "Mama? I'm hungry." Maya craved her mother's milk, but when the farmer took all the water away, it made her milk dry up.

"Get some water, sweetie. We'll eat later," her mother answered without thinking.

"There is no water, remember? What about milk?"

"Sweetie, you're gonna have to wait. You're a grazer now, and there's no going back to drinking milk."

"What if the hills don't have enough to eat?"

"The hills have enough to fill all of us up every single time we're there, and they have for centuries. Today will be the same."

"But what if the wolves come and chase us away?"

"Sweetie, Caesar will be with us, and they don't like Caesar. Besides, I've never seen a wolf up there. I've never seen a wolf, period. Trust me, you're going to be safe up there, and you'll get so full you'll wanna pop. There's alfalfa, flowers, grasses so long that even one single blade could fill you up. There's seeds and clover—oh, so much clover. There's wonderful weeds everywhere you look . . . roots, shrubs, leaves . . . you name it. Dry and dense with oils, or succulent and fresh . . . it's all there for you, I promise. Don't worry, love. You'll be fine and dandy and eating dandelions as soon as we're up there."

This chitchat between Maya and her mother woke up the others one by one. Edna was one of the last to wake up, and she did so in a sudden panic.

"Ahhhh! Billie!" she cried. "Where did she go?"

"Over here, Mama!" Billie called out, already wide awake and across the yard and by the gate that would later open up to the trail leading to the grazing hill.

Homer looked groggily at Edna with one cocked eye. "Good grief. It's the crack of dawn. Let's go back to sleep."

"First goat on the hill gets filled the fastest!" Doctor Sylvia said to Homer as she trotted by. She was headed right for the gate, where Billie was waiting.

"Hey, no cuts!" Billie said.

"Race you to the top!" Sylvia replied.

"Gate's closed."

"Well, when it opens then."

"Who opens it?" Billie asked.

While they discussed what was about to transpire in the next few moments, the other goats started to line up behind them. Other than Dante, the big buck, and Omar, the wether, every single goat on the farm was part of this crowd ready to race to the top of the grazing hill. They hadn't had water all night, so none of them needed to be milked, and every goat in the pen was hungry. The only task this morning would be to climb.

Suddenly the herd parted, and the farmer walked straight through the middle of them. He was headed right for Billie, and straight behind him stood a sprightly Caesar.

"G'day, mates," Caesar woofed from the other side of the herd, then he sat obediently, as was the routine for him and his farmer.

Billie looked at Sylvia and said, "Loser has to clean the winner's hooves."

"You're on, kiddo," Sylvia said, taking the bet.

"Where do you think you're going?" barked Caesar while looking Billie's way.

"To the top of the hill, and I'm getting there first."

"All right, all right, mate, but don't try anything devilish. The farmer and I will both have an eye directly on you, little Miss Someday, so don't go shooting through and taking some path off to Darkwood. You'd be caught before you can say billabong."

The farmer opened the gate, and suddenly Billie realized she didn't even know the way. How could she win this race if she'd never even seen the track?

"The winner always follows the beaten path," Doctor Sylvia whispered to Billie as she nudged by her.

Billie tried to get out of the gate, but she kept getting bumped to the side by the bigger goats forcing their way out of the exit ahead of her. She'd been pushed away from a good starting position and out to where winning was going to be nearly impossible.

"Hop on," Antoni said from somewhere.

Billie looked around for her friend, unsure of what she was suggesting. She saw Ovid coming through the pack.

"Hop. On," Antoni repeated herself. She was sitting on a nearby fence post, observing it all from above.

Billie figured out Antoni's advice. Ovid got close to her, and she leapt right on top of him, then hopped again onto one of the even taller adults, finally jumping down onto the well-beaten path that wound its way up to the grazing hill. The race was on.

Billie began trotting up the winding path, avoiding the flurry of hooves that shot back toward her as she raced, but there was little she could do to catch Doctor Sylvia by following the beaten path. She needed another way to the top if she was going to win. The path to the top zigzagged all the way up, so she thought she might try to cut out the zigging and zagging and make a straighter line.

Billie looked for opportunities, and a shortcut revealed itself to her. She took her little secret bypass, and it worked perfectly. She passed ten or so goats with just one maneuver, so she looked to do it again and passed even more. Before she knew it, she spotted Doctor Sylvia above her. Doctor Sylvia could see her competitor too, though. "Nice try, little one. It gets harder than you think, taking shortcuts!" She laughed loudly. Doctor Sylvia knew the shortcuts became more and more difficult as it got steeper. Not to mention how much extra energy it used up taking them.

Billie had gained some ground on Sylvia, but there were still goats packed together on the trail in front of her, blocking Billie from galloping up the beaten path. The good shortcut opportunities were drying up, so Billie conserved her energy and waited for an opening. The zigzag paths were getting longer and longer between turns, and if she ever found just one viable shortcut, she'd have to take a chance on it to be up at the front with the doctor.

"It's almost over, dear!" Sylvia shouted to her friend jovially.

"There!" Billie shouted and hit another shortcut. She got on to it, but this shortcut was very steep. A couple of sharp steps stole most of Billie's energy, and her breathing grew more labored. She took one last step and was back up on the trail with Sylvia, and this time Sylvia was behind her. Billie was in the lead.

The little doeling tried to get going and find a rhythm she could keep, but her energy was all but gone. She was gassed.

The doctor cackled as she passed the exhausted Billie. "Victory always follows the beaten path!"

Billie was trotting again but not nearly at the pace that she needed to catch the doctor. Her opponent was getting away fast. Another goat passed her, then a small group did. She searched for energy somewhere deep inside.

"Come on, Billie. Move your legs," she whispered to herself.

Her pace quickened, and she started to pass a few of the goats that had just passed her, but it was too late. Reaching the grazing hill first, Doctor Sylvia had a smirk on her face as she nibbled away at the pasture's offerings. She lifted her head briefly when Billie arrived and said, "I'll take that hoof cleaning when we get back to the farm." Then she winked.

"Double or nothing?"

"I don't think so, Billie," she said through her smirk. "I only bet on sure things."

"Oh my goodness! These are so good!" Maya shrieked.

"Have another bite, dear," her mother urged. "We've gotta keep filling up. If you get full, take a break, but it takes plenty of food and energy to be a proper goat! Try that shrub there—those are good for you." She lowered her head, following her own advice.

As the last goat reached the daily destination of the grazing hill, Caesar came trotting up behind Billie. "I see you made it, mate. If you can manage to stay within your grazing lanes, you'll do all right. Just head back down to the farm when I call it a day, and it'll all be easy-peasy for ya, mate. The good life."

Billie wasn't sure what to think of Caesar's extra close attention or his rules, but it was a clear day up on the foothills. The clear skies should have allowed her to try to get a quick glimpse at her ultimate goal: the Matterhorn. Unfortunately she found herself in a place where the view was blocked.

"Someday," she whispered to herself, knowing the mountain was somewhere back there, hidden by the trees lining the backside of the grazing hill.

"Forget about it, Billie. It's against the rules," Maya told her daydreaming pen-mate as she trotted by.

"Rules are for you and other kids, not for the greatest of all time," Billie said.

"They're for all of us, Billie. They keep us safe. Besides, who wants to be up there where there's hardly anything to eat or drink, no friends to make you smile, no one to rub heads with or rub your back. It all sounds awful up there to a perfectly normal goat like myself," Maya said.

"Some goats are willing to make more sacrifices for greatness than others, Maya."

"Risking everything isn't a sacrifice. Making milk for the farmer is a sacrifice."

"You'll never go where I'm going if you have to be milked by some farmer every day. I'm never gonna make milk because if you do, you can't climb up to the elevations I'm headed for."

"What's your deal with the Matterhorn anyway? It's just another hill. It doesn't really matter."

Billie turned and looked Maya in the eye. "It matters to me, and maybe one day it'll matter to you too. Maybe one day after I climb it, you'll ask me what's up there, what it's like to do something so amazing—maybe one day you'll wish you could climb it, but it'll be too late for you. I'll be standing there staring at you, and you'll wish you would've done something great like I did."

"You two break it up. We're all friends here." Sappho trotted up between them. "Maya, why don't you try one of these roots over here? Billie . . ." Sappho found a sunny patch of grass far away from Darkwood and nodded at it so Billie could follow her cue. "Why don't you try the grass over there in the sun? It's fantastic, love. You'll see what I'm talking about when you get there."

Billie trotted over to the grass her grandmother had suggested and started grazing reluctantly. Maya was still in her head. *What nerve she has, trying to dash my dreams. I don't tell her what to dream and what not to,* Billie thought.

Sappho walked over to her frustrated granddaughter and grazed side by side with her. "How'd the race go?" she asked.

"How'd you know we were racing?"

"We all overheard you and Sylvia. It wasn't exactly a secret. We all watched you give it your best, and I'm proud of you for that."

"Yeah, but I lost."

"The greatest doesn't mean you always win. It means you don't ever give up. It means you have too much heart to ever be stopped permanently." Sappho shifted so that she stood directly in front of Billie as she spoke. Billie's head was still down. "Look at me, dear. I mean it."

"Yes, ma'am." Billie picked her head up a little, but her eyes remained focused on the ground.

"I mean it. Look at me," Sappho said delicately.

Billie lifted her head higher and looked at her grandmother. When Sappho suggested the sunny patch of grass, she had known exactly what a goat could see looking up from there.

"Grandma?" Billie said, astonished by what her grandmother was showing her.

"I know, Billie. That up there is *your* goal. No one else's. Don't ever give it up. Find a way to make it happen, if that's what you truly want."

It was a clear day for miles and directly behind Billie's grandmother was the one thing Billie knew would unquestionably make her the greatest of all time: the summit of the Matterhorn. And because of where she was, it was closer than she'd ever seen it before.

Chapter 14

The afternoon shadows had grown long enough that Caesar had already called it a day up on the grazing hill, and all of the goats were back down at the farm again. All of the goats except Billie.

"Quit your lollygagging, mate," Caesar barked up at the idle Billie.

"I'm COMing—just one more SE-COND," Billie said for the umpteenth time.

She kept looking back to get extra glimpses of the Matterhorn on her way down. This must've been the twentieth time she had stopped by now. The next few steps she took finally put the peak of her obsession out of view. Knowing she wouldn't see it again on the rest of the way down, she headed home undistracted. Billie trotted all the way back from that point until she was through the gate and back on the farm. She didn't stop trotting until she reached a place in the pen where she could look up and see the object of her ambition again, though the sinking sun meant the view of it was fading. Billie also reminded herself of the race she had lost earlier and that she should train for tomorrow's competition if she wanted anything to change.

Billie was determined not to get stuck at the starting line again behind the adults. She looked for something to help her improve her jumping. She could easily hop onto Ovid or Kate to get where she needed to go, but they weren't necessarily going to be in the exact *place* she needed them to be *when* she needed them to be there. She knew she lacked the size to hold her place at the gate when everyone was pushing through it, but maybe she could work on being agile enough to hop onto the backs of the tall goats. That would allow her to force her way to the front by taking the high way to the starting line. She wasn't sure this strategy would work, but she decided she'd practice for it.

Billie looked around and noticed that the overturned water trough hadn't been set upright yet, so she ran right up to it and jumped on it as if it were a table. The trough was taller than Ovid but not quite tall enough to mimic the backs of the adults. She sat on the trough, looked around, and studied the pen. All the grownup goats had gotten their fill that day and needed to be milked, so they lined up to be helped by the farmer. The ones that weren't being milked still lined up to see if the farmer was giving out treats. It seemed to Billie as though he must've been giving them out, because several of the goats seemed to be taking something from his hand. They all looked content, even the farmer. When the treats were all gone, he led Billie's mother into the milking station. Billie noticed how happy she seemed doing her duty.

Crack! Billie whipped her neck around to find the noise. Virgil and Homer were locking horns, something goats do to find out who's stronger. All the kids did this from time to time, the adults too, and it determined the pecking order of who was who among them. Ovid was at the bottom, above him was Kate, and then it was Maya's crew and Maya on top of them for third place. Virgil and Homer were battling to determine who would be first and who would be second, but no one truly knew where Billie measured up in this pecking order of the kids. Games to determine that order annoyed her because her horns were so much smaller than the others', so she never got involved. Everything about Billie was smaller, frankly. She weighed less, had shorter legs, and had a little head and petite body, so she shied away from this sport. Standing on her trough, she looked around a little farther and saw Dante peering over his fence, enjoying a view of the little-league competition.

"Good shot, Homer. Leverage your momentum next time and push up with your neck. Virgil, try getting up on your hind legs and crash down on him. You're both doing great!" Dante coached from afar.

All the kids were circled around Virgil and Homer and watching this brutish but necessary competition. Billie jumped down off her trough-perch and marched right up to the kids circled around the horn-lockers.

"My friend, with such a grand entrance, is it a grandiose ending you seek?" Ovid asked Billie.

Billie didn't even acknowledge Ovid; she just trotted right past him and straight up to Homer, jumped on his back, and leapt off the other side of him.

"Hey, now! Watch what you're doing!" Homer cried.

Billie didn't say a word in response. She just kept walking through the circle and made her way toward Dante. Homer shrugged it off and prepared to launch his horns toward Virgil once more, but Virgil was rolling on the ground laughing.

"Haha! She hopped you! She hopped you so hard! Haha! That was brutal!" Virgil mocked his friend, who'd just lost the competition without even knowing what had happened.

Homer was shocked at first but started laughing with the

others, who were all cracking up at Billie's unexpected victory. Billie didn't see the humor in it—she just marched on toward the farm's largest current caprine member, Dante.

"I know I'm gonna be the greatest of all time someday, but how can I beat these big oafs at their game?" Billie asked Dante in frustration.

"I think you already have, kid." Dante was looking over the top of the fence while he motioned toward the scene of her recent victory.

Billie looked back and saw them laughing. "But they're all laughing at me, Dante."

"They're not laughing at you, kid. They're laughing about how you just hopped over the favorite. It looked like Homer was about to be the champion of the kids."

"I wasn't playing their game, though. I'm trying to win the race to the grazing hill tomorrow against the real big oafs, not my friends."

"That's right—you weren't even playing the kids' game, but you still bested their best with an undeniable show of dominance. That's all it takes. The point of it is to win the game, not beat them at their specific way of playing it. I'm telling you, you've got hutzpah, kid. That was fantastic!"

"It was? Fantastic?" Billie said.

"Look out, kid! Your reign is already being challenged!"

"Yup. Lookout, Billie," Omar the wether agreed.

Homer was charging toward Billie with his head down, ready to reclaim his position at the top of their pecking order. Billie turned just in time. Homer's horns were getting very close to her rump as her instincts took over. She leapt straight up, and her hooves found Homer's back again. When she felt the strength of her opponent's back under her, she pushed off and leapt again to avoid falling.

"Good one, Billie!" Ovid yelled from over in the kid circle. All the others were cheering too, but Homer had gotten up during the ovation and started charging again. Billie had to move out of the way again at the last second.

"What are you scared of, Billie? Face me! The challenge isn't over."

"That's not how it works, Homer!" Dante cried out as he laughed.

Billie made a break for it and headed for Story Tree Hill. Homer was hot on her heels, so she zigzagged back and forth, kicking up dirt to cloud his view and slow down his charge. Homer slowed down to let the dust settle. He scanned for Billie and finally found her at the foot of the hill, starting to climb. Homer made a beeline for the hill to challenge her once again.

"Come down and face me, coward!" Homer yelled up the hill.

"If you're so brave, come and get me!" she yelled back down it.

Homer flared his nostrils and charged uphill. This time Billie didn't move out of the way. As Homer started losing his momentum, she reared up on her hind legs and slammed down on his horns with a force Homer had never experienced being used against him in such a way before: gravity. His knees instantly buckled, and Billie stood over the buckling for all the world to see.

"Give up yet?" Billie stared down at the onlookers who had gathered to watch the scene.

Homer knew he had lost. "I give, Billie. You win," he said as he slunk down the hill.

Billie came down from Story Tree Hill and walked toward the other kids, but they backed away and lowered their heads as she got close to them. Billie had won the game she never really cared about, and now she was the top kid.

Chapter 15

"**G**et up, Homer. Get the others up, too," Billie said. It was still the wee hours of the morning.

"But, Billie, you've won every race for two months now. Can't we sleep in for once?" Homer replied.

"We've gone over this, Homer. We can sleep in when you best me, but until you do, I'll be training every day, so you and the others are going to help me. If I'm gonna climb the Matterhorn, I have to master the grazing hill. I can't master the grazing hill if the grownups block the path, so get up and get the others up, too."

Billie was at the gate before the rooster even had a chance to announce the arrival of the morning sun. As the seven other kids arrived one by one, she was slowly surrounded. Surrounding herself with the other kids was the best way she could figure out to secure her spot at the starting line. The adults liked to try to push to the front, but with the aid of the other kids, Billie was given the best chance to hold her place up front. It was getting easier and easier to hold it every day because the kids were growing bigger every day. They weren't fully mature yet, but you could see they were going to grow up to be healthy adults soon enough.

"You still owe me that hoof cleanse!" Doctor Sylvia teased Billie.

"You still owe me a shot at double or nothing," Billie returned with a smirk.

The farmer came out to the pen where he usually let the goats out to feast on the grazing hill, but today he didn't open the gate. He always opened the gate. He always milked the mothers, he opened the gate, the goats grazed, they returned home, he milked the moms once more, they slept, they woke up, and they repeated it all again. Every day he did this, every day the goats did this, but not today. Something was awry.

The farmer walked over to the gate, where the kids were surrounding Billie. He put a halter over Homer's head, then Ovid's, and he led them off in the opposite direction of the grazing-hill gate.

"Where is he taking you?" Billie asked during the commotion.

Caesar answered, "Settle down, mate. The farmer has guests. I think they want two new blokes over at their place." Caesar had seen this kind of thing before. Farmers from elsewhere would come here, and if they liked the little goats they saw, they would purchase them and take them home, and that was that. There was no need for him to question it; it was just how farms worked.

Billie was fuming. "Want them? They're my friends! You can't just take someone's friends!"

"Don't worry, mate—they're probably shootin' through today. They'll wait till the spring . . . after they've become wethers, most likely."

"They can't become wethers. That means they're sacrificed!" Billie said hopelessly.

Billie cautiously watched the scene. The two bucklings were having a grand old time with the new guests. They had brought human kids with them that got along great with Billie's buckling friends. They all seemed happy, but it bothered her. Something wasn't right. She still didn't know exactly what a wether was, but she remembered Omar was a wether, and she liked him. She thought, *It can't be that bad*, but was still unsure.

"Caesar, tell me the truth. What's a wether? What do they do to them?" she asked reluctantly.

"Oh, mate. It sounds terrible, but it's not the end of the world. They just make it to where the blokes aren't so aggressive. They can't have kids of their own either, but it'll all be all right in the long run, mate. Don't fret over it. The farmer knows what he's doing. You just keep following the rules of farm life, and farm life will be a peach."

Billie wasn't satisfied by the answer but felt as if there was nothing she could do about it now. She trotted over to where the bucklings were, but she was too afraid to get close lest they make her a wether as well.

"Ovid?" She tried to get her best friend's attention.

The farmer's little guests seemed to notice Billie and started talking about her, from what Billie could gather. The farmer seemed to be rejecting whatever notions the guests put forth about obtaining her, but she put a good distance between herself and these human intruders just to be safe.

When their visit was over, the farmer shook hands with his guests, waved goodbye, and led Ovid into the schoolyard barn. A moment later, he came back out and started inspecting the rest of his goat herd.

Homer trotted up to Billie after the farmer's guests left, but Billie wasn't having any of his cheerfulness. "What was all that about?" she asked.

"They were great! They're pretty friendly farmers, if you ask me!" Homer replied.

"Homer, they're going to take you away. That's why they were here."

"No, they're not. They just wanted to look at me. Ovid too, but they really liked me . . . I think."

The farmer now had Virgil in a halter and led him into the schoolyard barn too. Billie and Homer watched on in confusion until Ovid and Virgil trotted out, seemingly no worse for wear. But still, something happened to Ovid and Virgil that didn't happen to Homer. Billie didn't know what was going on, but it felt big to her. Everyone had already told her what she needed to know, but she hadn't yet pieced it all together. With the truth being hard to hear, none of them truly understood the flurry of changes about to occur in their lives.

Chapter 16

Peak winter was always long and harsh for the animals out in the wild, but it was long and harsh for the animals on the farm too, just in a different way. It was the first time for Billie and the other kids to experience it. For this and every winter alike, the inside of the barn would be the only scene they were truly intended to see for the entire frozen season. Over the warmer months, before it had gotten too cold to graze, the farmer had filled their place with plenty of hay. Now every animal on the farm with a hoof was packed into this wooden structure together, and the snow covered nearly everything outside. For the unforeseeable future, the locked-in life was to be their life. Not surprisingly, the whole situation made Billie stir-crazy, but she wasn't the only one.

The herd had been in the barn for so long that *every* member of the barn bunch had heard Sappho tell *every* story she had in the recesses of her memory, and she had told each one she knew at least four times over by now. In fact, at some point during the winter, nearly all of the goats became nominated to be unofficial storytellers. They would be asked to brew up their own tales and tell them to pass the wintertime. Ovid liked stories about the origins of things, Homer told tales of adventure, Kate's stories questioned tradition, Maya made observational commentary, and Dante even told an epic describing the seven circles of the underworld. When every goat on the farm had exhausted their story repertoire, some of the goats turned to Billie to ask for hers, but she told them, "I don't tell stories—I live them."

Billie felt trapped by the barn doors and the endless storms of swirling snow, but also by the inability to do anything about the inevitable departure of her friends. It was this impending goodbye more than anything else that made her feel so powerless. It sunk her spirits in ways she'd never felt before. Her mother encouraged her to become closer with Kate, a gesture of empathy from her point of view. She knew exactly what was likely to happen to Billie's buckling pals, and knowing what it would do to her daughter's friend circle, she wanted to soften the impact on her daughter. Kate just adored Billie, so it seemed like a match with possibility. Actually, it was the only possibility, because Kate was the only doeling that didn't seem to resent Billie.

The problem was that Edna's daughter had never bonded with any of the doelings. In her early stages, she mostly just stuck to herself, tolerated the company of Ovid, or enjoyed the competitively spirited moments with Virgil and Homer. The little doelings that Billie was growing up with spent all of their energy talking about what others were doing rather than focusing on themselves. That drove a wedge between Billie and the other doelings. Hair talk, their social competition, and focusing on others' opinions just had a naturally repelling effect on her.

Their barn had an elevated area to store extra hay, and there was a gradual ladder leading up to the storage mezzanine. There were low trusses, high trusses, low beams, and high beams and all kinds of objects to climb throughout the barn. Outside, it was a fortress covered in snow that could neither be infiltrated nor escaped by anything with proportions larger than a feline's, so the hooved inhabitants lived safely within the barn's boundaries.

Early on, the other kids challenged Billie to perform various stunts they came up with, but every dare that they could conjure for Billie had already been exhausted. Their coerced stay in the barn had become mundane, and boredom filled their days.

Over time, Billie decided that the best place to wait out winter was on the high beams that the others couldn't reach. Only Antoni joined her up there, and that was only when Antoni wasn't hunting mice. The cat was the opposite of stir-crazy, though. She was kept busy chasing mice out of their warm fortress, which constantly summoned the little pests in from the freezing cold. Every new strategy the mice thought up to enter the barn kept Antoni's job interesting, but Billie didn't have anything to do in that barn other than survive until the next day. She longed to see the Matterhorn again and to start another race to the top of the grazing hill, or to practice shuttle runs up and down Story Tree Hill.

"I dare you to jump from the high beam to the low beam," Homer said up to Billie in the rafters one afternoon.

Billie didn't answer. She sat there on her beam steadily, staring off into nowhere.

Antoni came to her defense. "She's already done that. Twice! Think of something new." Antoni was up on a high beam just across from Billie, staring off into nowhere in a matching posture, but instead of the look of defeat on Billie's face, Antoni looked highly in tune with her environment. Anything that moved was of absolute interest to Antoni, and virtually nothing in the world interested Billie.

"Stand still, kid," the cat whispered to her friend.

Antoni leapt over her friend on the high beam, went past her, then slipped over the joists that held the wall up. Her tail was whipping back and forth with a tight rhythm behind her lowered profile to hide it from her victim. In a split second, she burst into pursuit, sliding through a ventilation flap and chasing a furry rodent out onto the snow-covered awning. Billie wasn't impressed. She didn't even turn her head to watch.

"What if we did that?" Ovid said from below.

"Did what?" Billie asked dryly.

"What if we found a way to escape like the furball?"

"All the doors are locked."

"We're goats," Ovid said. "We can escape anything we put our minds to."

"Now, why would you want to escape?" Edna intervened, as if being cued. "You have everything you need in here. Just wait the winter out, kids."

"Wait? What are we waiting for?" Billie asked.

Her mother replied, "For spring? Warmth from the sun and the green growing things? For our normal lives? Surely those are worth waiting for, Billie."

"You mean our normal lives where our friends get taken away and our normal lives where we get stuck in here all next winter too?"

"Well, it's a whole lot better than being out there starving and cold. Besides, the farmer knows what's best for us. I just wish you'd trust him like we do. He's not out to hurt us. He needs us just as we need him."

"He's just using us. What about what we wanna do? What about *our* dreams? What about the things *we* care about?" Billie had taken a lot of time to think about their lifestyle while being stuck inside these walls.

"The farmer has given me my dream," Edna said. "You're my

dream, Billie, and you're wonderful. You're more than anything I could have ever hoped for."

"Did you hope I'd be best friends with a bunch of bucklings that will get sent away? Did you hope I'd be all alone?" Billie asked rhetorically.

"Billie, you're not alone. I wish you could see that."

"Yeah, Billie!" Ovid said, looking up. "I'm still right here. Come on down and hang out with me."

There was no sadness in Ovid's voice, and it lifted Billie a little. She leapt across to the low beam, then to the elevated hay loft, down from the mezzanine on the gradual ladder, and joined Ovid. Ovid had been sitting next to Edna, and he stood up upon Billie's arrival. He head-butted her haunches from out of nowhere and ran off.

Ovid had picked a playful fight, and Billie wasn't one to back down, so she chased him around in the little finite barn. It wasn't long before Billie caught him. He had run right toward Virgil and Homer, then lain down in the hay.

"I yield, I yield!" Ovid said with a smile.

"All right, Ovid, what gives? That was weird," Billie said.

Ovid looked at the other bucklings. "All right, kids, we all know what's going to happen. The farmer's getting rid of us."

Homer replied, "Yeah, but that family seemed really nice. If we have to leave, at least we get to go somewhere nice where they'll take care of us."

"You can't guarantee that, Homer. What if those human kids grow up and get mean like Dante?" Billie said, knowing exactly who was within earshot.

"Hey now, I resemble that remark," Dante said as he picked up his head.

"Come on, you guys—we're goats. We can escape anything."

Ovid revealed the priority of this whole scheme. "We're friends forever, right? And if we want to stay together, we have to get out of here before the farmer gives us away."

"And how are we going to escape, Ovid?" Billie asked.

"Count me in," Dante said, without being cued or even considered.

"How do we count you in if Ovid doesn't even have a plan?" Billie asked Dante.

"I don't know. Just count me in. This barn is driving me crazy!" Dante groaned.

Suddenly, the cellar-style doors were flung open. The bright sun reflected off the snow and into the barn through the opened doors. The farmer stuck a hose into the trough down through the cellar-style doors. It was a clear day, and it was the farmer's usual pattern to fill the trough on clear days, so they had somewhat expected to see him. He walked over to the ice-covered hand pump, broke the little bit of frozen water that had formed on it, and started filling the trough with fresh groundwater. Before they knew it, he was done. He slammed each of the doors back down, barred the horizontal doors shut with the solid piece of wood that went across them, and went back to the house.

Several of the does got up and enjoyed the fresh water. Dante watched them for a long while and noticed them start to hook their hooves on the side of the trough and stretch their necks downward as the water level lowered.

"There's our way out," Dante said. "Right through those doors, then out to freedom."

"Yeah, but the trough's blocking the way," Virgil said.

"I'll take care of the trough, but we'll need your feline friend to help us with the barred cellar doors," Dante said, looking at Billie. "Then we can escape this winter prison."

"That's a pretty big board holding the doors down, and she's just a cat," Billie said.

"Just ask her to take a look and see what she can do."

"How are you taking care of the trough then?" Virgil asked.

Dante rose slowly and cracked his giant neck. "Just watch."

The giant long-haired buck walked over to the trough and took a huge drink from the vessel. He motioned for the bucklings and Billie to join him. They all started drinking.

"Hey, no fair! You're hogging all the water," Maya's friend Phillis said.

"Be our guest," Dante told her as he gave up his place at their little reservoir. "Please, drink as much as you'd like. We can certainly make room."

Phillis got her fill and lay back down in the hay bed she'd been lying in before. Dante took her place when she finished and started drinking again.

"What about me, Dante?" Ovid's mother said, batting her eyes.

"Well, of course, m'lady," Dante obliged cordially.

Soon all the goats were taking turns lowering the water level, but eventually they all had their fill, and the trough was still too heavy to move. Dante wasn't worried, though—he just started head-butting it with his enormous horns. The water was sloshing back and forth.

"Oh! I gotcha now!" Homer said and started butting the trough every time that Dante did. In fact, their head-butts were nearly in perfect sync. The other bucklings did this too, and in no time, the water was alternately splashing out of either side. Dante head-butted the trough one more time and stopped. He studied the waves and figured them out. As the waves splashed up on his side of the trough, Dante hooked his tremendous hooves on the lip of the vessel and pulled.

"Oops," Dante said, grinning as the water spilled all over the barn floor. "My bad."

"It's okay, Dante," one doe cooed.

"It's perfectly fine with me," another doe said.

"Don't worry about it, Dante."

"I don't mind, Dante."

The does all echoed the same sentiment, and Dante was forgiven immediately.

"I don't know how you put up with such a clumsy buck like me, everyone. My apologies for the mess. Perhaps you'll forgive my carelessness."

"Not to worry, Dante. We can all understand your frustrations," said Doctor Sylvia.

Preferring not to be wet, the does within the spill radius all rose and found dry ground where they could lay back down. "Ovid and Billie, could you do me a favor and check behind the trough? I'm afraid we've knocked it over. If you'll push it on over here closer to me, I can fix it," Dante said.

Billie and Ovid got behind the trough and pushed. Dante helped them push it farther out, then turned the trough over completely so the bottom was now the top. It was the same trough Billie had used to practice her jumping ability when she was younger. The very same one she jumped off of when she crossed the yard to get advice from Dante about being the best and ended up besting Homer. Dante walked into the area they had cleared. After some rearranging, the clearing was just below the cellar-style doors.

Dante said, "Let's see what happens when I do this."

He got up on his hind legs and punched upward with his great horns. One of his horns was on each of the doors as he pushed, but the action was stopped by the bar on the other side that held them together. Billie and Ovid watched, looking at each other when they noticed the crack that had briefly formed between the doors.

"The next step is getting Antoni's help to knock the bar off." Dante demonstrated the motion he wanted Antoni to complete for them with his horns, as if they were a conductor's baton.

Ovid said, "I don't think we need her. Billie's horns are small enough to fit through the crack if you can hold the doors open for a few seconds."

"And how is she going to get up there high enough to put her horns through the crack?" Dante replied.

"On your back," Ovid said.

"And let her best me? I don't think so."

"It won't mean a thing once we're free, Dante," Billie said.

"It'll mean something to me, kid. My pride, my position, my everything. The plan's off unless you have another way to escape."

Dante's demeanor changed from upbeat to cheerless. He dropped his head, angrily withdrew from the situation, and went back to the bed of hay he had claimed before this whole plot got started. He lay down, exhaling a cloud from his humungous lungs. From there, he stared blankly at the post right in front of him until he fell asleep.

Chapter 17

It was late into the night, and Billie just couldn't sleep. She was still thinking about the escape plan that got canceled. "I've got an idea," she whispered to Dante.

"Go back to bed, Billie," Dante said.

"Everyone's asleep. No one will see you doing it, Dante. No one will see me doing it. We escape, I'll submit, and you're back on top. No one will ever know what I did for even a second!"

Dante looked around, slowly coming to grips with this idea of Billie's. Everyone *was* asleep. He paused in thought, then reluctantly said, "All right, but don't you dare wake anyone up. And not a word of how this happened."

"I promise. Cross my hooves, hope to die, poke a hay needle in my eye. Not a word."

Dante walked over to the cellar-style doors and pushed them up with his horns until the crossbar stopped the action. Billie got up on the trough that they had turned over earlier, then hopped onto Dante's wide back. When she was settled, he got up on his haunches and pushed the cellar doors up with just enough force that Billie could see through the crack. Billie steadied herself for the task as she thought, *His back is as sturdy as solid ground.* She looked around to make sure the others were still asleep. Looking up, she stared through the crack. It was definitely big enough to get one of her horns through. She stuck her left one underneath the crossbar and slid it up until it teetered off her horn over to the left side and slid down. The doors were no longer being blocked.

"Push again," Billie whispered.

With the crossbar gone, the doors were unimpeded; now they just needed to fully open them so they could escape. Billie hopped off of Dante's back so he could finish the job. With one great flick of his horns, he swung one cellar door open, then the other. The fresh snowfall dampened the sound of the doors being opened, so no one seemed to be alarmed yet. He got back down on all fours and looked at Billie.

"What are you waiting for?"

"Are you sure you're okay with this?"

"Just do it already," he whispered.

Once again, Billie hopped from the trough to Dante's back, then leapt to her snowy freedom. As soon as she was up and out the door, she was followed by Ovid, then Virgil and Homer. They were not quite as asleep as Dante had believed. Dante shook his head, knowing he had been duped. He swallowed his pride, putting his bulky hooves up on the clearing and climbing out to his own snowy freedom. He looked back at the warm space that had confined him all winter and started to worry about the others they were leaving behind. He knew the barn would cool off quickly, so he closed one of the two cellar doors.

"Just in case we have to come back this way," Dante said to his cohorts. "And it'll keep them a bit warmer too."

Regardless of Dante's effort, the barn would cool off quickly with even just one door being wide open. The bucklings, Billie, and Dante made their way toward the back gate while the sleeping does were woken one by one by the invading frost. Billie could hear conversations inside the barn growing louder as they got closer and closer to the back gate. This very same gate led to the grazing hill and to a world without fences.

The moon was glowing off the snow, and the stars twinkled all over this reflective ground covering. The snow was so high they could barely see the top of the fence posts. The height of the snow made it difficult to travel through, but Dante was packing the snow underneath him as he made his way toward the snow-covered gate. All four of his kid comrades had to use the path he forged to walk along the otherwise impossible passage.

Wham!

"Oww!" Dante shouted, halting in his tracks. Billie ran into the back of him and caused a pileup of kids behind her.

Dante kicked about softly and nudged with his horns, trying to understand the obstacle in front of him. "Ah . . . that must be the gate." He paused. "And it looks like we're on a mound right here—we only have the one rail to clear!" Normally, there were three rails.

Dante put his hooves up on the highest rail and leapt over the fence without a problem. He turned and blocked the way for the others with his massive horns.

"What kind of trick is this?" Ovid demanded.

Dante was staring right at the black, white, and brown little doeling. "Billie, do you submit?"

Billie hadn't thought about her promise, but the words of submission got stuck in her throat.

"I'll submit," said Ovid.

"Then come on through," Dante replied.

"Move over, Billie," he said before he jumped past Billie and on to the grazing-hill side of the fence.

"Me too! I submit!" Virgil said as he followed his friend. He looked back at Billie from the side of freedom. "Why aren't you submitting, Billie?"

"I submit to you, Sir Dante," Homer said and made the jump.

Billie tried to jump over the gate, but Dante knocked her back with his horns.

Dante said, "It's nothing personal, kid, but a promise *is* a promise, and what good are you if you don't keep your word?"

While the escapees delayed at the gate with this game of submission, the bleating from the barn grew loud enough to wake Caesar. Caesar barked to alert the farmer, and before Billie knew it, she could see the lights in the log cabin flip on. It was now or never.

"I'm still the greatest," she said.

"Nope. This makes me top goat again," Dante replied, staring at her unbudgingly.

"Fine. I submit. Like I promised, but just to you. Not to them," she whispered.

"And I accept." Dante looked back across the gate. "Well, come on. We've got an adventure to go on!"

Before Billy even crossed, Dante raced up the hill. "Last one to the top is the dirty rotten haystack!"

Billie leapt the gate, and the race was on. Cold air constricted her breath more than usual, but she made ground on the others quickly. They all seemed to be impacted more by the weather than she was.

Before long, she had hopped over or around all three bucklings and was now up front with Dante. She couldn't really pass Dante because of the deep snow, but it thinned out some the higher they climbed up the path. At times, the wind blew clouds of frosty powder off the hill, clearing some of the snow on the path, but while the gusts made her way look easier, it also challenged her balance.

Billie suddenly slipped a little, and her heart skipped a beat.

What were they actually doing, escaping from the safety of the barn and the farm too? The realization hit her like a ton of stones. Here, they were all free to do what they wanted, but with this freedom came bitter cold and a path that was difficult to stay on. She had no idea what they would even eat, where they'd find water, or if they'd be able to stay warm.

Billie wanted to climb the Matterhorn. She wanted to see where the mountain goats roamed and the bighorn sheep reigned, but she knew she was just on the path to the grazing hill at this point, and she couldn't even see the Matterhorn. In late summer, she could see it from this same place. In the fall, she could see it even though snow mostly covered it, but this winter season was a different beast. How could she use her mind to figure out where to go next if she couldn't even get a glimpse of the biggest thing around? What information did she have to go on?

The goats slowed their pace. "This has to be the grazing hill, right? It gets a bit flatter when you get to the top, right?" Ovid asked.

"I think you're right," Billie said.

"Well, what's next?" Dante asked the others. "I've never been here, you know."

"I don't know. I'm hungry though," said Homer.

"Yeah, me too. I worked up an appetite," said Virgil.

AH-OOOOOOOOOOO.

AHHH-OOOOOOOOOOOOO.

AHH-OOOOOOO.

The cacophony of howls came from all directions. Dante and the tallest bucklings looked around anxiously, but there was little to see in this pale moonlight. Billie and Ovid looked around as well, but they were too short to see over the snow embankments.

Then . . . Dante spotted them.

Chapter 18

"**F**ollow me, farmer! Follow me! I have the scent! Follow me, farmer! They're up there, farmer. I can smell 'em, mate." Over and over again, Caesar yelped at the farmer on the way to the gate. The farmer stopped when he reached it. He was dressed for the harsh winter, with his gun in hand and Caesar at his side. He inspected the situation at the gate, seeing all the tracks and where they led, then he looked down at his Aussie.

"They went over, farmer! Look at these tracks! Look, they went over, mate! They've gone over—let's go!" Caesar barked frantically as he leapt the back gate and looked back at his master. "Let's go get the goats! Come on! Come on!"

The gate was sandwiched by the snow in such a way that when the farmer tried to swing it open, it wouldn't budge. The farmer looked back at the barn and saw the cellar door wide open. He stopped his pursuit of the escapees, walked over to it, and closed it patiently.

"Come on, mate! They're over here! Don't worry about the does! Over here! Over here! Over here!"

As soon as the methodical farmer turned his attention back to the gate, the dog tried to lock eyes with his human. Finally, the two connected, and Caesar knew the farmer would see where he was going. The farmer was going to hop the fence and follow Caesar.

"I'll get 'em, mate! Here I go! Here I go! Here I go!" Caesar was unquestionably intense. He ran up the hill, and not long after, he was followed by the farmer, gun in hand.

———

Dante had just spotted something suspicious and whispered, "Nobody move. If that thing notices us, we're dead."

There was a gray figure moving across the grazing hill near the edge of Darkwood. It stopped and sniffed the cold air. It was a wolf. It trotted back and forth, nose in the air, trying to get another whiff of their scent.

"I don't think it sees us," Virgil said with his statuesque head positioned above the embankment.

"I don't either," Homer said, tracing the wolf's movements with his eyes.

Dante said, "Either way, don't move. Wait until he stops looking this way, then we'll backtrack until we're hidden. If we get back to the trail, we can follow our tracks. And if we get back on the trail, don't look back until you're home. I'll be right behind you, if this goes well."

The goats heard Caesar barking at the farmer from somewhere far away. The wolf could hear it too, but it wasn't acting as if it was alarmed by the shepherd dog.

"Can we leave now if it can't see us?" Ovid's angle prevented him from seeing the wolf.

"Don't, Ovid. It'll hear you if you move," Virgil whispered, still staring at the gray beast.

With Billie's view of the wolf blocked by the banks of snow, she looked off in a different direction than the others. She noticed a dark figure far off in the distance, climbing a fallen boulder. The boulder sat just at the edge of Darkwood, away from where the wolves were. The shadow figure had a stoutness about him that somewhat reminded her of Homer, but this character was far bigger than her adolescent friend in every way. Powerful shoulders made climbing look absolutely effortless for the shadow. In two or three moves, the figure made it to the peak of the boulder, then it just stared across the grazing hill, taking it all in.

Atop the boulder, the moonlight illuminated the staunch figure more than when it was climbing. It was looking down at the wolves. He had a rack of horns that did not curve upward like Dante's but spiraled backward and around. *This must be the bighorn sheep my grandmother told me stories about*, she thought. One of the great rams from the mountains! She was finally seeing one with her own eyes. It had to be a ram, if not the alpha that ruled the Matterhorn. Staring fearlessly down at the gray apex predator, the ram suddenly turned its head toward the five goats. The ram locked eyes with Billie, and it felt to Billie as if they had an understanding. It sized Billie up, looked back toward the wolf, then back at Billie. It paused with his eyes on her again and slammed his hoof on the boulder one time.

SSCLACK. CLACK. Clack . . . clack.

The sound echoed as the ram stood poised on the boulder. Virgil noticed the wolf's attention shift from the smell in the air to the crashing sound of hoof and rock coming together. "Let's go," he whispered.

Dante motioned with a flick of his head toward the trail and whispered, "Go, kids. Now."

Billie didn't move right away. She got up on her haunches and looked for the wolf beast she'd only heard stories about. She noticed one slinking in the general direction of the sound that the ram had made. Billie began to understand that these apex predators had fallibilities, and she felt more confident about herself being in this wild world. She thought, *Even those that rule struggle to find their way.* But before she could complete the thought, the wolf changed direction and started slinking toward the goats.

Dante noticed the wolf. He breathed in deeply, deciding what he should do. Then he flexed his powerful shoulders and twisted his head on his neck. He'd fight if the time came. All the while, the wolf crept closer.

SSCLACK-SSCLACK. CLACK-CLACK. Clack-Clack . . . clack-clack.

Still positioned on the boulder, the ram cracked both hooves against stone this time. The wolf stopped its advance and turned toward the sound. Unfazed by the beast's attention, the ram slapped his hoof down again, letting the wolf know it was no accident. The wolf found the ram with its eyes but didn't give chase. It just stared back, lifted its snout into the air, puckered its mouth, and howled.

AHHHH-OOOOOOOOOOOOOO.

Other wolves from all over answered.

"Go, Billie," Dante told her.

Billie got down off her haunches and back on all fours. She could still see the ram. She scraped the ground with her own hoof somewhat, mimicking the actions of the bighorn sheep, but hooves in the snow didn't make much of a noise, especially compared to the sounds the ram made. She looked down and scraped again at the snow, clearing a patch.

"What are you doing? Get out of here. Those wolves will be here any second." Dante implored his little friend to take action.

Billie looked at him as he ran past her. She brazenly got back up on her haunches to see what the wolf was doing again. It was still relatively close to the goats but facing away now. Billie lowered herself and looked up again toward the ram. It was still poised, unafraid of this moment. Billie wasn't afraid either. This was no time to panic for either of them. This was a time to make good decisions.

AHHH-OOOOOOOO.

Billie looked back down where her hoof had scraped the snow and noticed the shrub beneath it. Here in a field of icy despair, there was still a sign of hope: a shrub fighting to live through winter. She looked up at the ram one more time, and he flicked his head at her. *Another sign*, she thought. Billie took the ram's advice and headed down the trail.

She tried to catch up to her little herd quickly and quietly. The closer she got to her friends, the louder Caesar got, but then his barking stopped.

"Where did he go? Where's Caesar?" Billie asked Dante.

Dante stopped his descent and looked around for Caesar. "I don't know."

The entire situation was transitioning from scary to eerie. When they had hopped the fence, the plan had seemed so straightforward: Live free. It felt as if they had taken control of something, and now they were completely controlled by an enemy they couldn't see. An enemy that owned their every thought and action.

"What was that?" Ovid said when he heard the snow crunch in front of them.

"Behind me, kids," Dante ordered.

The crunching of snow continued, and it kept getting closer. The kids were all huddled tightly behind Dante, fearing the worst was yet to come. Then came a growl as a gray silhouette leapt over the trail out in front of them. The kids buried their faces in the thick fur that covered Dante's torso while Billie stepped forward to get a look at the inescapable adversary that was approaching.

"Farmer!" Billie yelled out.

The farmer stopped, raised his gun to his shoulder, and aimed at something over Billie's head. The farmer was shaking as he squinted one eye. Billie was sure that the farmer was aiming at Dante.

"No! Dante didn't do anything wrong! It was me!" Billie cried at the farmer.

GRRrrrrrhhhh.

Billie turned when she heard the growl coming from behind them. The gray wolf that had found their scent on the grazing hill was now upon them, zigzagging down the trail. A second growl came from the left. Billie glanced over and saw a second wolf. She looked around for an escape route. There was a narrow path peeling away from the main route. It looked too dangerous, but it was probably even more dangerous for wolves than goats.

The wolves seemed unconcerned by the farmer. They must not have seen him aiming his gun at their shadows. Suddenly, the second wolf saw an opportunity and lunged at Virgil, his mouth open and ready to clamp down. Virgil tried to move away from the beast, but there wasn't anywhere to go. The wolf was about to close its jaws on Virgil's haunch when a strike of fur-filled fury launched across the trail from out of nowhere.

"Caesar!" Homer cried out.

Caesar and the wolf both slid to a stop and repositioned themselves. The fight would've gone on, but farmer fired his gun into the air, startling everyone but Caesar.

POWWWWWWWWWWWWWWWW!

"These are my goats! You and your mates best be off! Cowards!" Caesar yelled at the retreating wolves.

The ring of gunfire echoed well after Caesar stopped yelling at the wolves. When they were all out of sight, he yelled, "Leave and never come back, ya bunyips!"

"Thank you, my Caesar," Virgil said when his nerves had settled. Not a hair on his head had been touched.

"All of you bogans without a lick of sense do exactly what I say, or I'll put a nip in you you'll never forget." Caesar ignored Virgil's words of gratitude.

"We were fine. All your barking at the farmer nearly got us killed," Billie snapped at the shepherd dog.

"You keep believing that, ya dongo," Caesar said sharply. "Them bunyips are no more scared of you than you are of a handful of hay, and you're here acting like a darn fool who's lost half her brain out here."

"You weren't there. You don't know," Billie retorted.

"Didn't have to be, dongo." Caesar cocked his head. "What were you trying to do anyway? You have all the food, water, and warmth you need back in the barn. Up here it's cold, there's nothing to eat, and them bunyips make it dangerous as Hades."

"The farmer is gonna take my friends, so we took a chance at freedom."

"What are you gonna do with freedom, Billie Someday?"

"Live," she said without hesitation. She looked back up to the boulder where the bighorn sheep had been poised. The ram had vanished without a trace.

Chapter 19

The last evidence of another harsh winter had melted some time ago, along with Billie's heart. As she anticipated, Ovid and Homer were swept away by the farmer's guests. Omar and Dante disappeared too, but without a hint of their destination. Virgil was the new wether now, isolated in the pen with the farm's newest guest buck; they mostly kept to themselves.

If Billie wanted to talk to Virgil now, they had to yell really loudly because of the distance, and neither was the loud type. The farmer had moved the fence between the bucks and the does farther apart than it ever had been before. He must have felt it necessary to keep his new buck an extra distance away from his herd of does after the escape. Because Virgil was the farm's wether in the buck pen now, that escape stunt moved Billie's only childhood friend left on the farm even farther from her. As a result of the changing state of affairs, despair crept into her mind. Every once in a while, over the fence, Billie could hear Virgil getting along with the new buck like grass and flowers, but joining their conversation required raising her voice. It was almost always too much effort to chat; when she did, words were often misinterpreted, meaning was lost, responses were slow, and connections usually fell flat. Real face-to-face conversation with old friends was all but gone for Billie. It felt as though she lived beneath a rock.

She didn't really have a single hooved friend anymore, when she thought about it—certainly not any like the friendships she enjoyed with the bucklings as little kids. She still enjoyed talking to Sappho from time to time, but that was her grandmother, not a friend her age. Antoni also had conversations with her occasionally, but even Antoni was often aloof.

Billie thought the one thing she would still enjoy was the morning race to the grazing hill, but Caesar ruined those. He followed her up the hill and made sure she paired up with a tattletale doe, then he'd follow her all the way back down the hill at the end of the day, right on her heels and insulting her all the way down. It wasn't until she was inside the gate and the gate was closed that he relaxed at all. His overbearing commentary weighed on her. He blamed her for the escape attempt, even though it was Ovid's idea too. He shamed her dream of climbing the Matterhorn if she even so much as glanced at it, and he regularly reminded her that he'd "saved her life" when the wolves had her and her mates trapped. Every single time Caesar was anywhere near her, he reminded her how wrong she was about it all. Wrong, wrong, wrong. Everything she did was wrong. She couldn't even make a simple climb to the grazing hill without messing something up.

"Ya slip there, dongo?" Caesar said to Billie after she kicked a rock. "If you slip up on one of your dream cliffs up there, it's bye-bye bogan-bogoat. Better to be down under in the valley with us, mate."

Billie was a bit surprised by this. Caesar was still being critical, of course, but he hadn't called her "mate" since the winter wolf stunt. She thought he might be letting up on her, but one kind word was all she got that day. All his patience for her left the farm from the cellar-style doors she had escaped through, and it was probably never coming back, no matter how welcome it would be.

Doctor Sylvia told Billie that Caesar's onslaught was coming from a good place, but how could someone put you down so deeply if they actually cared? Virgil would yell for her to keep her head up, Edna told her to just do whatever Caesar said, Sappho encouraged her to endure, and Antoni told her to act as if it were nothing. Antoni said that if she acted as if nothing happened, then, eventually, it would feel as if nothing happened. Ultimately, no one's advice worked. This was *her* life. She needed to decide what *she'd* do about it, and *she* needed to respond in the way Billie Someday would respond.

"Have you ever slipped, Caesar? Ever?" Billie asked as they hiked to the grazing hill together.

"No, I don't believe I have, dongo. Besides, if I slipped, who would watch over these obedient does and keep all the good ones safe?" he said.

"Sure you have. You've slipped up," she said. "Remember when you couldn't even watch after a few little bucklings and doelings in a schoolyard, and one of them escaped into Darkwood? Or how about that time five goats left the farm, escaped the barn, and made it to the grazing hill? You were supposed to make sure they stayed in the barn, right? Sounds like you've slipped to me."

"All right, dongo, what's your point?" he said.

"Caesar, it seems like a waste of your valuable time to follow me up and down the mountain when you've gotta look after each and every single goat on this trail, am I right? That is your rather important job, isn't it?"

"Most important job on the farm."

"Well, for a goat like me with good balance like I've got, this is no big deal. It's simple hiking. If I slip with one hoof, I have three other hooves ready to do the job and catch me from falling, but that's not the case with you. There's only one of you, and you spend all your most important time watching just me. What if something happened to one of the others while you're watching me?"

"The farmer found a good one in me, ya hear. No bloke in this world could've done this job *this* well. Most shepherds don't have what it takes to monitor such a big hill alone like I do on this grazin' one."

"I don't disagree, Caesar. You do cover a lot of ground. You keep the predators away—you do it all—but these days you're focused on just me. I'll make you a deal, seeing you've got such a big important job looking after our entire herd. If I see *any* other goats trying to escape, I'll be the first to tell you. I'll even go help you find any escapees. In fact, if I see them escaping, I won't stop looking for them until they're safe again under your watch."

"I don't need you to tell me how to do my job, and I certainly don't need any help from a rascal," Caesar snapped.

"Caesar, what if I tried to escape five times a day and tried to convince others to go with me each time? Maybe I don't get away every time, but one time I probably *would*, and what do you imagine the farmer's gonna think of you then? If I escape a third time, what happens to you when he finds out?"

"All right, Billie, what are you asking for?"

"Simple. I just want to be trusted to climb to the grazing hill alone. No one bothering me about it. Not you, not another goat, no one. And when I get to the top, I'll pair up with whomever I wanna pair with. That's all I'm asking for."

Caesar stepped off the trail onto a ledge, sat down, and panted heavily as he worked to catch his breath. Billie kept going but then realized he had stopped. She looked back at the tricolored Aussie.

"If I get kicked off this farm, it's gonna be your fault, you know?" Caesar quipped from his ledge.

"That wasn't my goal, Caesar. Never was." Billie kept climbing slowly and turned back. "If a goat tries to escape, I'll be your number-one doe, boss. Your right-paw doe," she said, knowing they'd reached a deal.

"You better, kid."

"I'm not some kid, remember? I'm Billie Someday, the greatest of all time." She walked without saying anything for a bit. "And you have my word."

"All right, you climb the hill by yourself, but if I pair you up with someone, you pair up with 'em. No earbashing."

"Deal," she said.

———

Billie waited at the top of the hill until Sappho arrived. She felt relieved being able to climb to the hill in solitude for once, and now that she was with the majority of the herd, she didn't want some wayward goat approaching and spoiling her mood. Being forced to hang out with Maya, Kate, or any of the other goody two-hooves from the farm felt as if it would sabotage the good vibes she was currently feeling. She had plenty on her mind, and Sappho was always present, willing and ready to listen if Billie had something to get off her chest. So she waited patiently for her grandmother.

"Spill it, child," Sappho said, looking up at her granddaughter as she arrived. Billie had watched her wind back and forth up the path all the way to the top of the hill, and Sappho knew patience of this kind from Billie meant she was loaded to the horns with goatly concerns.

"I will, but can we go over here first?"

"Okay, love, lead the way."

Billie got to a spot where she thought the others wouldn't be able to hear her. She looked around until she was sure everyone had their heads down, grazing.

"Grandma, this way of life just isn't for me. I mean, having kids and supplying milk and doing whatever everybody else is doing, that's not for me. I feel like I need to leave this farm. I just know there's something better out there for me. I need to chase my dreams."

"It's one thing to talk about it, and another to do it. Your friends are gone and living their lives. You know you have to live yours too, now."

"I know, Grandma."

"No, Billie, I mean it. You're not the type to dream up dreams, then not follow them. I'm not either," Sappho said.

"What do you mean you're not *either*? Were you a dream chaser when you were younger, Grandma?"

"Well, yes, I guess I was. When I was a doeling, my grandfather was still on the farm but only for a short time. He had grown too old to go through rut, so the farmer took him out of the buck pen and let him into the schoolyard pen with us. He was very patient with us and played our little kid games with us. Once a week, he sat us all down in the barn and spun us a magical tale. When he told stories, all the kids sat and listened eagerly. He drew an audience in and dangled them from the tips of his horns with his words. His stories helped shape us into who we'd become, because his characters felt so real that they became important to us. It was almost as if the characters themselves *were* us. You'd get so lost in his stories that whatever lesson the character learned, you learned it too. It was amazing what he could do with a captivated audience, with little minds that were truly listening."

Sappho trailed off a little and left Billie room to speak up. "What happened to him?"

"Well, all of a sudden he was taken from us. After that, we were all devastated and wanted our storytelling friend back. We all craved a storyteller, and suddenly I knew just what I wanted to be. I needed to be that storyteller. I told everyone I was going to be a storyteller just like my grandfather, but no one took me seriously. They didn't take me seriously because I was a doeling. The bucklings knew they could grow up to be storytellers if they wanted to, but doelings weren't allowed. There wasn't a good reason why—does just didn't do it back then. I thought I could be different and prove everyone wrong. Prove to everyone that a doe could tell stories just as well as a buck could."

"Well, you did, didn't you?" Billie exclaimed.

"You're right, Billie, I did. But that doesn't mean it was easy," Sappho replied.

"Why wasn't it easy? You just tell a story like you do now, and everybody likes it, right?"

"For generations, only bucks told stories, and we does were forbidden. That was our society, our way. We gossiped in the pen or out on the hill, but no doe was given the spotlight. I wasn't allowed to have the attention of so many, but there was something in me that didn't care about the rules. I had to figure out a way around the rules until the rules changed."

"What are you two going on about?" Caesar butted in, followed by Kate and Maya.

"Are you planning another failed adventure, Billie?" Maya asked.

"Yeah, you're not going to try to do something *cool*, are you?" Kate asked.

Maya looked back at her friend Kate with a questioning look. Kate must have felt the peer pressure of her friend's stare, because her words didn't match her tone.

"Cool stuff is so lame." Kate tried to recover.

"Maybe this time you could take ten of us with you to get eaten by the wolves. That would double your old record," Maya prodded.

Caesar finally got around to making his point for this confrontation. "We're breaking up the pairs. Billie's going with one of these two, Sappho."

"Why are we breaking up the pairs?" Sappho asked Caesar. "Everyone's behaving."

"You two haven't had a single bite up here," he replied. "You're just talking it up. Time to eat."

Sappho looked down at her granddaughter. "Billie, why don't you go with Kate? I'll pair up with the lovely little Maya."

"But, Grandma . . ."

"Just trust me, love," Sappho replied. "I'll see you back at the farm."

"We'll have fun, Billie," Kate said. "I promise."

"That depends on what you call fun," Maya said sharply.

"Come on, Maya—I can show you some grass way over here that you've never tried. It'll make your coat glisten all summer," Sappho coaxed her new partner.

"I need to work on my elegance. What can I graze on that's best for elegance?" Maya asked.

"Oh, we'll have to go way, way across to the other side to work on elegance," Sappho answered quickly.

"Kate, be a good mate and watch this dongo for me . . . closely," Caesar urged.

"No problem, Caesar," Kate replied as Caesar trotted off.

"Don't let her talk you out of your good sense, love." Caesar said his last piece as he trailed off.

"You don't have to watch me, Kate," Billie told her newly arranged partner.

Kate waited for Maya to be out of earshot. "Billie, I'm not like her. She's just being mean because she's insecure."

"I wish she'd try to hop me in the pecking order. She'd regret it instantly if I showed her a thing or two . . . ," Billie said.

"Billie, she just takes some sort of issue, you know? But that's just *her* thing. I think you're pretty awesome."

"Thanks, Kate, but I'm really not feeling that way lately. And if I start feeling like I am, Caesar will call me *dongo* again like it's my birthright, and I'm right back to being a nobody."

"Don't listen to Caesar, and don't listen to Maya. You'll always be somebody. You've been somebody ever since I can remember. Billie Someday, you just need another adventure to remind you of who you are."

"Maybe, but how can I go on one with that dog on my haunches all day?"

"Well, we can work on that. Caesar trusts me . . . but do you trust me? Because I think I might be able to help with that."

"Help?"

Kate stared at her friend with softened eyes. "I could help you, but only if the next plan has a more delicate way about it."

Billie didn't answer Kate, and Kate didn't pry any further, but a seed was planted in Billie's mind: *Kate might really actually be my friend, and she wants to help.*

Chapter 20

The herd had all had their fill on the hill, the sun was low in the sky, and each goat had returned safely to the farm for the night before the last of the sunlight. Caesar was doing his late-evening walkabout, circling outside the fence and checking for weak spots; Sylvia and Edna were gossiping with the other grownups; Maya and her two cliquish friends were standing on the boulder up on Story Tree Hill, talking about their futures in farm society; and Sappho was huddled up with Kate, discussing something important. At least important enough that they looked intense from afar. Billie certainly thought they did.

Most evenings when Billie came off the hill, she kept to herself in thought or practiced climbing maneuvers discreetly, but today she felt a bit like talking. She looked around and studied her conversation options. There was grownup gossip and doeling dealings, she could get in a friendly long-distance yelling match with Virgil in the buck pen, gab with her grandmother and Kate, or run the inside loop of the fence while receiving slights from Caesar from the outside of it. Then, from the corner of her eye, she spotted the cat crossing their pen. She decided Antoni was her best bet. Billie trotted up to her.

"Don't get too excited, Billie. I'm just a cat. An extraordinary cat, but still a cat," Antoni said somewhat defensively.

"Yeah, but you're also my extraordinary friend, right?" Billie said.

"What makes you so excited to see me?"

"I think I've got something really big coming up," Billie said.

"Well, do you or don't you?" Antoni asked.

"I don't know. I just need the ear of someone I trust."

"I can see you need to chat, but a goat passed me an urgent message from Sappho," Antoni said, "and I'm headed over there. So, gotta thing, gotta go."

"Oh . . . ," Billie replied, her head drooping a little.

"I'm pretty sure you're invited," Antoni said.

Billie lifted her head, but she was still apprehensive about speaking her mind around Kate. Kate was with Sappho at the moment, and knowing who Kate's pals were gave Billie pause.

"Are you coming or not?" Antoni asked.

"Oh, uh . . . yeah," Billie said reluctantly.

"Don't act like that, kid. This is *for you.*"

"For me?"

"Come on—you'll see."

As Billie and Antoni approached Kate and Sappho, Kate was chatty, but she quit talking the moment she realized Billie was coming over.

"Billie," Sappho said after they arrived, "you and Kate need a chance to start over. A trusting friendship could be good for both of you." She looked back at Kate, who was trying to appear small behind her. "I know you've met, but let's just try this. Kate, this is my granddaughter Billie. Billie, this is my dear friend Kate, and I think you two would make good friends."

"Hi, Billie," Kate said sheepishly.

"Hi, Kate."

"And, of course, you both know Antoni," Sappho said.

"Hello, kids. Hello, Sappho. Now that that's over, why am I here?" Antoni asked.

"Billie may not know it, but she would like some help accomplishing a special feat, and she would like that help to come from both of you."

"Grandma, I don't need help," Billie objected.

"See, Sappho! We can't help someone that doesn't want help. So, are we done here?" Antoni shook her head. "Youthful arrogance rears its ugly head yet again."

Billie wanted to climb the Matterhorn, and at this point, everyone on the farm had heard her or someone else say she did. She knew in her heart that this was what she wanted, all of them at the meeting knew it, but Billie the kid wouldn't accept that she needed help to make it happen. All four of them knew there were obstacles to it happening. Antoni knew she would have two of them before she could even get started climbing and knew Billie had no plan to get around them. First, she needed to get away from the herd without Caesar catching her. Second, she'd have to cross Darkwood without being harmed, and that's before she could even start climbing the actual Matterhorn. Her one experience with wolves nearly ended the lives of six perfectly good farm goats. The truth was, Billie needed a plan for everything if she was going to climb this mountain, and she hadn't even considered planning the first step, much less the second, third, or fourth. She had been so low since the bucklings' departure that she hadn't had a clear thought in months, and as her confidante, Antoni knew this all too well.

Sappho broke the tension. "Perhaps I can share a helpful story: My story is about becoming a storyteller." The three audience members were certainly receptive to a Sappho story. "I started to tell Billie about this earlier, but I didn't get a chance to tell the *whole* story. I didn't tell her *how* I became the storyteller you all know today. You see, when I was a kid, does and doelings were not allowed to tell stories. Only bucks and bucklings were."

"Why not?" Kate asked.

"Well, Kate, I can't answer that because I had the very same question myself back then. *Why not?* Why *couldn't I* tell a story? Why were only bucks and bucklings doing the storytelling? I could feel stories inside me that needed to come out, and I knew I needed to share them with the world, but my world shunned this idea. I didn't know why. It turned out that there wasn't a good reason for why—it's just the way it used to be. But just because *certain* things are a certain *way* doesn't mean that they can't change. However, change requires a catalyst."

"What kind of cat?" Antoni asked.

"No, no, Antoni. It's not a cat necessarily. I guess a catalyst could be a cat, but it's 'a being that gives rise to change.' I was the catalyst for does and doelings being able to be the storytellers we are today. However, change doesn't always take root. Sometimes a grassroots-level movement has a bad grip and slips and falls, never to rise again. This means that catalysts need others to keep them from slipping. Meaningful change in farm society needs others to join in with the effort for that change, and that's the part where you come in." Sappho gave Kate and Antoni a look. "I believe Billie is a catalyst for change. I don't know what this change means for others, but I believe this farm needs it, and Billie needs you, or she'll end up being the slipping catalyst that never found her grip."

"Grandma, I'm not trying to change the farm," Billie chimed in. "I'm just trying to be myself."

"Billie, you mean to climb the Matterhorn and return to the

farm, but you don't believe this would bring about change? That's not realistic, love. Your stunts have already led to changes around here. How would the biggest stunt ever pulled off by any goat anywhere not change the farm?" Sappho asked.

"I guess I haven't thought about it that way," Billie answered.

"How do you plan on leaving the farm with Caesar's eyes constantly on you? How do you plan to cross Darkwood unscathed?" Sappho asked the questions Antoni had as well.

"I'll figure it out. I always do," Billie said.

"For a goat that's hung her head so low lately, you sure do lack humility," Sappho said.

"I have humility," Billie said.

Antoni spoke up. "You have fields of courage, mountains of confidence, and rivers of gusto, but you don't have one grass blade, pebble, or drop of anything that adds up to something resembling humility." Antoni was surprised by her own bluntness.

"Billie, if I didn't have help when I was coming up, I wouldn't be able to tell stories like I do today. When my grandfather passed, I tried to tell stories to my mother, but she shunned me. I tried to tell them to the doelings my age, and they said it was against the rules. The bucklings made fun of me for trying. My brother was part of that buckling group, but he didn't tease me. He waited and watched for the others to leave, and when they were gone, he asked me to finish my tales. He knew it was forbidden, but his love for me eclipsed any allegiance he had to the rules. Regularly, the two of us found time to sit down for another tale. Eventually, my confidence grew. I got better at telling stories, too! I would get quiet as a mouse to develop tension, then burst into the climax to build excitement. One day, my outburst got us caught. Everyone on the farm knew what I had done, and they all shunned me for it. Everyone but my brother."

"What did your brother do, Sappho?" Kate asked.

"Well, Kate, my brother continued to encourage me. He convinced one of the bucklings that my stories were good. Then one day, instead of just telling stories to my brother, I told stories to two bucklings, then three, and then the doelings surrendered and joined the story parties, too. My brother convinced the entire herd that if the farm's buck gave it a listen and approved, the rules should change forever. The buck listened, and he loved my story, and now I'm known by everyone around as a storyteller. Even mountain goats living in the highlands got wind of my tales, and some have even showed up at the farm to hear them from time to time. And it all started because I trusted my brother to help me."

"Yeah, but for stories, you need someone to listen. To climb a mountain, I just need the mountain," Billie said.

"Slow your heart, Billie. There is nothing but love among us here. Remember, you already tried to climb during the winter, and you know that doesn't work. That means you're going to have to try to do this during the summer. If you can't figure out a way to get away from the herd and away from Caesar this summer, then you'll have to wait until next year to try," Sappho said. "And maybe next summer it's the same thing again, and there goes another year. And another, and another, and maybe you *never* make your dream happen because you never let others help. This is how a maybe dream becomes a *never* dream."

"Never?" Billie hadn't thought about the possibility of *never*.

"Or maybe you could accept help, achieve your dream, and be remembered forever for who you truly are," Antoni said. "It's not like we're climbing with you. This will be *your* climb, just with a little of our help at the start. I can probably get you through Darkwood. It won't be easy, but you could use a set of instincts like mine out there if you're gonna get through it."

"And I can get you away from Caesar without anyone being able to do anything about it," Kate said.

"How would you do that?" Billie asked.

"A distraction and maybe some confusion," Kate said confidently.

"How would you create a distraction?" Billie wanted clarification.

"We could argue about it," Kate said.

"Argue about it?" Billie was still confused.

"Yeah, argue about it *like* a *loser*," Kate replied.

"Like a loser? What's your idea?"

"Don't worry—we'll get to that," Kate said.

Chapter 21

Billie was never much for argument, but on this day, she would need to learn to argue and argue quite loudly for their plan to work. If she wanted to climb the Matterhorn during this lifetime, she'd have to accept her changing world and work with the various snags that were in front of her. Her conversation the day before with Kate, Antoni, and Sappho might not have taught her everything she'd ever need to know about life, but it did show her who she could trust and who she couldn't. Almost every member of the farm, other than her cohorts, was untrustworthy in matters of an escape, and that much was crystal clear.

"Move over!" Kate yelled at Billie, who was crowding her at the starting gate, determined to win. Morning had arrived, and a race to the grazing hill was about to take place.

"You move over! This is my spot!" Billie said, loudly enough for others to hear.

"Looks like you have some competition today, Billie!" Maya called out.

The arguing got Maya's friends' attention. Phillis whispered to Emily privately, "When did Kate decide to challenge Billie?" Then she yelled for the crowd to hear, "You can take her, Kate!"

"Not too sure," Emily quietly replied to Phillis's question, then cheered loudly, "Beat her good, Kate!"

"Hurry up, Caesar!" Billie yelled at the herd dog. The tension was palpable.

"Hurry up? You know the farmer lifts the gate, but I'll tell you what . . . seeing you're in a race today, I'll let it go," Caesar replied to Billie, then looked over at Kate. "Good luck out there, kid, but you gotta keep a close watch on Billie for me, all right, love? Don't let her run off."

"No worries. She's always too tired to go anywhere after a race anyway," Kate yelled back.

"Well then, good luck, speed racer. Do your best," Caesar replied.

The farmer walked over to the gate, and Billie's excitement grew. She hadn't raced in quite some time, so she thought this little competition with Kate would be a good warm-up for greater things to come. The farmer lifted the latch, Kate pushed Billie as hard as she could, and Billie went down. Right down to the ground. Before she could even cross the starting line, she was off her hooves, unable to get started, and her challenger was already building a sizable lead.

"Good luck, dongo!" Kate yelled out from her first-place position.

Billie got up off the ground and muttered, "'Dongo' might have been a bit much." Then she joined the herd of grazers making their way back and forth along the winding path to the grazing hill. She had memorized all the most efficient shortcuts and so had Kate. If she was going to come from behind and make an effort to win this race, she'd have to run it nearly perfectly. It helped that most of the does didn't know Billie's shortcuts at all, so she could easily pass them, but getting into first would be highly unlikely with her having started the race back so far, thanks to her pal Kate. She found herself in third place well before she expected, and right in front of her was an old adversary: Doctor Sylvia. She thought, *This will be fun.*

The problem with Doctor Sylvia was that she was familiar with every shortcut that Billie was. There was no easy way around her, so victory was slipping further from Billie's grasp. The last and most challenging shortcut neared as Billie watched for what Sylvia would do. Sylvia looked as though she might not use it, but she did. Billie made a split-second decision, doubled her speed, and took the long way around.

Billie gained on Kate, but Sylvia finished her shortcut, staying in second. Billie was still in third, and Kate was pulling ahead up front. The shortcut had worn Sylvia down, and Billie still had fresh legs. She caught up to Sylvia easily enough, and it was on to chasing Kate. However, Billie's victory wasn't to be this time. Just as she passed her old adversary, she heard the victory cry of her new adversary from up above.

"Yes! I win! I win! I win!" Kate shared her victory with those that could hear, then raised her voice even higher. "I BEAT BILLIE SOMEDAY!" The victory cry echoed all the way down the mountain.

Sylvia could see Billie in front of her with her head hung low. The poor thing. Not only had she lost all her buckling friends, but she'd also lost her grip on being the best of the bunch. Little sweet Kate broke Billie's victory streak, and from Sylvia's vantage, Billie looked devastated.

"I'm sorry, Billie. She really did you in back there," Sylvia said. "But keep your head up—you'll get her next time."

Billie muttered, "It might be a while."

The rest of the herd began to arrive one by one, and each

paired up with a grazing partner. As they arrived, every one of them said something to either Billie or to the victor, then got on with the daily grazing, but Maya was different. She wouldn't let it go. Neither would her friends Phillis and Emily. After all, they believed their dear friend Kate had just made important farm history.

"We knew you could do it, Kate!" Phillis cheered.

"You had her the whole way!" Emily hailed her friend.

"Billie Someday, I think I know what the 'Someday' part of your name means. It means that 'someday' Kate will beat you! Because she just beat you . . . TODAY!" Maya tore at Billie's heartstrings. "She's champion now! Kate's the new boss!"

"That doesn't make her champion!" Billie cried, sounding as genuinely angry as she needed to. "She cheated!"

"She didn't cheat—you're just a sore loser," Maya said sharply.

"She pushed me over before the race even started!" Billie defended herself.

"It's all part of the race—she won fair and square," Maya said.

"Billie, I don't weigh that much. You just weren't ready for a race today, so I won. Congratulate me, and maybe I'll give you another chance to beat me tomorrow."

Billie turned to the little goat that had just beaten her. "I doubt it. You're too chicken to try me!"

"Settle down, settle down," Caesar said, getting in the middle of the word squabble. "I'm guessing she beat you, huh, dongo?"

"Yeah, but she cheated. You saw it," Billie declared. "Everyone on the farm saw it. She humiliated me in front of everyone!" She was nearly in tears.

"Billie, it's not the end of the world. Calm down, sweetheart," Edna said.

Caesar said, "It's not my race, mate. I don't get involved in races—I get involved in goats taking their proper places. Now you two pair up and have a post-race brekky together like old mates."

"I'm not pairing up with her," Billie said.

"Why not? I thought we were friends, Billie," Kate said.

"Not after you cheated me we're not."

Kate said, "I don't mind that you're like a loser. That's not my problem."

"Fine, you two break up your pair," Caesar said. "Billie, you're with Maya. Kate, you're with Phillis."

"But I'm always paired up with Maya," Phillis said.

"Well, I'm breaking up your pair. You just do as you're told."

"Caesar, the pairs are working great for us. Phillis and Maya, Kate and Billie, and Emily and I," Edna said. "We don't need to change anything. It's working fine the way it is."

"Miss Edna, I'm sorry, but I can't be with your daughter any-more if she's going to call me a cheater. I'll pair up with Emily today."

Sappho entered the circle. "Edna dear, I could use a chitchat with you. I need to discuss a little matter of health with you."

"Mother and daughter, you two set off then," Caesar declared. "Maya and Billie, you two set off that way. Kate and Phillis, you that way. That leaves Emily and only Emily."

"I can't be alone. Who do I go with?" Emily asked.

"Fine, you go with Billie and Maya." Caesar's decisions had been finalized.

"Great, now Maya and Emily are going to gang up on me," Billie groaned.

"Maybe you'll learn how to be a proper goat with *our* influ-ence," Maya said.

"Enough! You all get going. Get something to eat before the day ends," Caesar said. His patience had worn thin.

Billie hadn't even had a bite to eat that morning, and she already knew she had to find herself a new grazing partner. As she trotted toward a shrub patch with Maya and Emily, Billie had her head up looking for another quiet partner to graze with instead of being the odd doeling in the trio. All the way over to the shrub patch, she was forced to listen to them speaking unfavorably about her.

"I wonder if Billie will ever be the same after that last race?" Maya asked.

Emily said, "If that was me, I'd be *devastated*."

"I mean, what goat has such bad balance that little ole Kate can knock them to the ground?" Maya asked.

"I know, right?" Emily said.

"ENOUGH!" Billie yelled. "I'm gonna graze with Ovid's mother if you two don't stop."

"Stop what, Billie?" Maya asked in a tone intended to taunt.

"Can I graze with you?" Billie yelled over to Ovid's mother, who was a ways off.

Ovid's mother was still in mourning after her son's departure. She didn't even have the energy to reply; she just nodded, lowered her head, and allowed Billie to join her. Maya left Billie alone after that. Even Maya and Emily weren't cruel enough to be mean in front of Ovid's mother after all that she'd been through with losing her buckling. So now Billie finally had a good place to wait *it* all out in peace.

"Can we eat over here?" Billie asked Ovid's mother. "I don't want to be anywhere near Darkwood."

Ovid's mother nodded, and together they moved farther away from where the others all congregated.

While Billie separated herself from her nuisances, Kate was on the other side of the grazing hill, stirring up a magnificent manifestation among the others. "How did you do it, Kate?" Phillis asked in a high-pitched voice.

"Really, it was quite simple. I was just the best. I started the race, and I knew I was the best. I finished the race, and I still knew I was the best. The best simply knows she's the best when she's the best, so I didn't stop to question it. But now that you bring it up, I guess I should explain how it all happened."

"Please do!" a goat from her audience said.

"So there I was—"

Sappho stopped Kate in the middle of her story, her expression purposefully deadpan. "My understanding is that *there* you were and *there* you cheated my little Billie. So here I am, calling you out, Kate, you menacing little show-off."

"It's my story. You get to tell all your stories. How about you let a little goat have a chance at telling hers for once? You're being a meanie!" Kate improvised.

"Whoa now, you two. Calm down," Phillis said.

"Don't try to calm me down! I won that race fair and square, and Sappho is trying to steal all the glory from my story!" Kate shouted.

"THIS ISN'T WORKING!" Caesar snarled at the arguing foursome. "You. Kate. You're with Edna. And you. Phillis. You're with Sappho now. Find your own places to graze and leave each other be. I'VE HAD ENOUGH!"

All the goats quieted down immediately after Caesar's display. He was always barking orders, but never quite like this. Kate's mouth dropped open. She should've expected this to some degree, but the plan was working perfectly. She was with Edna now, and that was the plan.

"Sorry, Caesar. I guess this is just one of those days, isn't it?" Kate said calmly, then trotted off with Edna behind her.

"Be a good goat and go get your fill, Kate," Caesar said in a kind way that demonstrated the soft spot he had in his heart for Kate. "The day's been won already."

"Not yet, it hasn't," Kate mumbled to herself, but Edna heard her.

Billie's mother replied with a whisper, "What do you mean 'not yet'?"

"Can you keep a secret?" Kate asked as they moved toward an area somewhat close to Darkwood on the backside of the grazing hill.

"Of course," Edna replied.

"Billie has escaped," Kate said.

Edna panicked. "My Billie? No! Billie! No, this can't be happening again!"

Edna thrashed about, turning her head everywhere to look for Billie, but her daughter was nowhere to be seen. Edna ran deep past the edges of Darkwood Forest, screaming for her child again and again, moving farther from the safety of the grazing hill: "Billie! Billie!"

Kate followed Edna and started yelling, too. "Billie escaped, everyone! Billie escaped!"

Other than Billie and Ovid's mother, who were on the other side of the grazing hill, the entire goat herd and their shepherd dog turned into a flurry of commotion. Organized panic ensued in a way the herd had never experienced. They were all on the same page and acted as a group. When they looked over to where Kate and Edna were, they thought they were watching Billie run up into Darkwood Forest. They thought it was Billie trying to get away, but it wasn't Billie. It was Edna. Billie was nowhere near Darkwood Forest. She was enjoying a calm moment with Ovid's mother, filling up on flora before her journey, and no one saw her or knew where she was except Ovid's mother. Billie made sure that was the case.

There were only two goats on the farm that looked anything like the black, brown, and white Billie: her mother, Edna, and her grandmother, Sappho. And it just so happened that when they all looked toward Kate and Edna, it appeared that Edna was Billie and that Billie was trying to make an escape. Caesar sprinted toward Edna faster than he'd ever run before.

"Billie Someday, GET BACK ON THE GRAZING HILL RIGHT NOW!" Caesar cried.

Edna turned toward Caesar. "Where did she go? I don't see her!"

Caesar stopped in his tracks. "I thought *you* were Billie."

"Where did she go?" Edna asked.

The herd followed behind the galloping Caesar, trying to find the missing Billie. But Billie was expecting this fuss and walked to the middle of the grazing hill to announce herself and her innocence. "I'm over here!"

Caesar, Edna, Sappho, Maya, Maya's two friends, Doctor Sylvia, and almost every other member of the herd (minus Kate) turned toward Billie. They saw where she was and galloped over to her. They were whipped into a frenzy and needed to solve this mystery. All of them needed to figure this out for themselves, all of them except Sappho, Kate, and Billie. They had created this mystery, after all. Kate stayed next to Darkwood Forest during all the commotion and was secretly creeping away now that everyone was focused on Billie.

"Where did you go?" Edna asked.

"She didn't go anywhere. She was with me the whole time," Ovid's mother said, vouching for Billie's whereabouts.

"Is that true, Billie?" Caesar asked unnecessarily.

"Yes, I never went anywhere. I've been on the grazing hill all morning," Billie answered dryly.

Out of the corner of her eye, Billie saw her friend Kate walking up a hill through Darkwood, followed closely by Antoni. They were escaping, and she knew the plan would work as long as Caesar fell for one last dupe.

Step 1 of the scam was to lose the race so they could argue over it and both get new grazing partners. Step 2 was to get everyone to believe Billie had escaped by framing Edna. Step 3 was to reveal she had never left. Step 4 was for Antoni and Kate to escape together unseen. But for step 5 to work, Billie needed to buy just a little more time to convince Caesar of his part of the plot. Caesar's love for Kate was his weakness, and they planned to use it.

"Why did you think I escaped?" Billie asked Caesar and the herd.

"Everyone heard Kate yelling that you escaped, and your mother was looking for you," Maya said.

"Well, did you find me?" Billie asked.

"Obviously," Maya said.

"Can we go back to grazing now?" Billie asked.

Caesar said, "Yeah, yeah. Everything's all right. Let's get you sheilas back grazing again."

Billie watched Kate and Antoni disappear from the herd's view. "One more thing . . ." Billie waited to garner Caesar's full attention. "Kate was the one who said I was missing, right?"

"Yeah, what's your point, Billie? Are you gonna call her a *cheater* again?" Maya asked.

"No, she won fair and square. I just don't see her. Where'd she go?"

"Kate?" Caesar called out. "You're somewhere around here, aren't you, love? Speak up, mate."

No answer came. All the goats and Caesar looked around for Kate. It was so quiet that you could hear a grasshopper jump.

Billie finally broke the silence. "Well, she's nowhere to be seen. If she's escaped, I promised you I'd help find anyone who's escaped. Didn't I, Caesar? Where'd you see her last?"

"She was just at the edge of Darkwood over by Edna." Caesar was dismayed. "Edna, did you see her?"

"I don't know. I was focused on my Billie," Edna said.

"She must be in the woods then. I've been in Darkwood before," Billie said. "So I think I'll be the goat you'll want with you anyway."

"Yeah, mate. I'll take you. Ready to go back in there?" Caesar asked her.

"Ready as I'll ever be."

Chapter 22

Caesar held his nose high in the air as he tried to locate a scent. Billie's eyes were peeled, looking for signs, but she was also focused on the sounds of the forest. The pair made little to no sound of their own. Before she and Caesar left, she told him what to expect: The forest always listens, an alternate escape plan is a must, and there would be no chance to speak in there. They'd use signals instead.

While Caesar's nose was in the air again, Billie spotted a tuft of hair on the ground. Without a doubt, it was something that got pulled off of Antoni. The hair on her belly caught on all kinds of things. Billie covered it up with a bit of debris before Caesar had a chance to see or smell it. You see, they weren't truly tracking Kate in the traditional sense. Billie already knew exactly where they'd be meeting—the spot where the gray cliff spiked up above the trees.

It was the only reasonable meeting spot anywhere in Darkwood. The cliff looked too steep for a wolf to climb, making it appear relatively safe, plus it was the only object in the woods they could easily identify from the grazing hill. The cliff was the natural choice for their plan. The only one, really.

Billie led Caesar to a path where she thought there should be hoofprints in the dirt from Kate. Caesar stopped on the path and sniffed the air yet again. Billie signaled Caesar with a scratch from her hoof, and he immediately looked over at her. She motioned down, pointing at a hoofprint, then motioned again for them to go up higher from where they stood. Caesar agreed with a nod, and up the trail they went. It wasn't long before their quiet climb concluded at the cliff's base.

Caesar stopped and looked around. Down below him he could see the sharply angled forest floor with sparse tree cover, and above him there was just the cliff. There was almost nowhere to hide in this environment. From this vantage point, he could easily see most of the beaten path that slithered up to where they were. The dirt path's worn condition told him they were not the only ones to have ever taken this route. Lots of wildlife must have taken it as well, right up to the cliff. Greenery was scattered throughout the area, although when he looked up at the cliff, it was nothing but sheer rock edges that were going up, and up, and up. With little to no greenery on the cliff, it looked uninviting to him. He could walk along the base of it a bit farther if he needed to, but continuing upward wasn't likely to get him very far because, among the athletic skills Caesar possessed, rock climbing was not one of them. He could do a little of it if he had to, but not very well. He was awkward, unlike Billie, who seemed as if she was in her element up on a cliff face.

Caesar put his nose into the air again, and everything seemed normal—even safe enough to whisper, "Well, mate, what now?"

Billie whispered, "It might be too steep for you. I can go up and get Kate by myself, if that works for you?"

"Of course, mate." He sniffed the air again after agreeing.

It was the scent of a wolf. He looked around in panic and spotted it: a lone wolf. *At least it's not a pack of them*, he thought. It hadn't spotted them up on the cliff yet, and it was sniffing around as well, trying to pick up a scent of its own. For the time being, Caesar had a little bit of an advantage, having spotted the wolf before it spotted him, in addition to the wolf being upwind from them. He practically sprinted up the hill in fear after deciding the beast was headed their way.

Caesar was on Billie's heels in a flash. She had no clue what the panic was about. She found a ledge high above the dirt path for them while Caesar looked back down the cliff to see what the wolf was doing. Billie followed Caesar's glare to see what had startled him. There it was—Billie spotted the lone wolf.

Its head was low to the ground, and it was sniffing constantly as it trotted toward their ledge. Its eyes were low enough that Billie knew she hadn't been spotted, so she kept her gaze fixed over the edge, looking at the beast. Caesar did the same. It was better to know the wolf's intentions than to be stuck up on a ledge waiting for a surprise attack. As the wolf got closer to the cliff, Billie could see more of the beast. Its fur was a mixture of white, gray, and brown. Its long bushy tail was kept straight behind it as it trotted along its course with its black nose low to the ground. Its golden eyes had *relentless* written on them as they searched for something live to lock on to.

Getting closer to Caesar and Billie, it still hadn't looked up yet. Then, the wolf halted, lifted its head slightly, and crouched its posture to match where its head was pointing. It looked as though it meant business now. It started sprinting up toward their cliff. Billie pulled her eyes away from the ledge and braced herself.

"Don't fight it. This'll be quick," they could hear the wolf saying.

Billie looked at Caesar, and Caesar looked back at Billie.

Eek eek . . .

SNAP!

Billie suddenly realized that they weren't the wolf's target, so she peeked back over the rock ledge. The wolf was holding a marmot in its mouth that it had just nabbed. It was almost as if the cliff were a tree that the wolf was picking fruit off of.

"I know you're up there," the wolf told Billie and Caesar. "You're lucky I already caught my meal. Don't let me catch you around here again, or I'll have you hanging from my jaws instead of this guy." It knew more about its surroundings than they could have ever guessed.

"You won't," Billie said courageously. "You'll never catch Billie Someday."

"And who is this Miss Someday?" the wolf replied. "I haven't smelled your kind around here before."

"I'm the greatest of all time, so get moving. I'd be a waste of your time and energy," Billie said, still hiding.

"We might have to see about that . . . but that can wait for later. My pups need to eat, so I'll be taking this marmot back to my den. You're welcome to join us if you'd like!"

"You're cunning, wolf, but I'm not that gullible," Billie said.

"It's Mrs. Wolf to you, and suit yourself, but we'd love to have you for supper!"

"Not on your life!" Billie yelled out fiercely.

"Don't let me catch you in here again then." The wolf craned her neck, looking up. "Well, if you're the greatest of all time, can I at least get a look at you? I wouldn't mind seeing what the greatest looks like."

Billie revealed herself.

"Well, for a mountain goat, you sure are small," Mrs. Wolf said.

"She's a farm goat," Caesar said. "And she's coming back with me."

"Well, get on with it then. Ta-ta for now! Good luck getting through my forest!" The wolf trotted away, marmot clenched between her teeth.

"Wait!" Billie shouted. "What about your pack? Where are they?"

The wolf stopped and put the meal down that she'd nabbed for her pups so she could answer without a full mouth. "They're up north of here, trying to settle a score with a ram."

"Well, good luck to them! I hear rams are tough to beat!" Billie remembered the ram that distracted the wolves that day in the snow.

"I agree! A very worthy adversary he is," the wolf replied, then picked up her pups' meal and trotted off.

Billie waited until the gray wolf was gone. "She was friendly!"

Caesar didn't answer for a while, but then he suddenly started singing, "D-O-N-G-O, D-O-N-G-O, D-O-N-G-O, and Billie was her name-O." He stopped singing and said, "So, is this what it's like to hang out with *the* Billie Someday on one of her big adventures?" There was a flare of admiration in his tone.

"You're darn tootin' it is, Seeze-O," Billie said with an air of confidence, before putting on her serious face. "Look, I know it seemed stupid to talk to Mrs. Wolf, but I figured the more information we got from her, the better off you'd be on the way home."

"Maybe you know more than you let on, mate."

"I do, mate. I'm pretty S-M-A-R-T . . . smart."

Billie marched forward up the sharp rock face, and Caesar followed suit. It wasn't long before Caesar had trouble balancing on the side of the steep cliff.

Crrrckkk. Catta Catta CATACATA chrrrrr.

Billie looked back from an overhang at her climbing partner, and he was clinging with all fours to the side of the cliff, creating a rockslide beneath him. He fidgeted until he found a place to rest all four paws safely.

"Caesar, I can do this by myself. It'll be safer if you wait," Billie said.

"Yeah, you go on ahead, mate. Safety first," the dog replied.

"She's just up here."

"Just go, mate. I'll be here," Caesar said through a heavy pant. He was relieved he didn't have to go any farther.

He looked down and saw how far he had come chasing Kate. Caesar was a hundred feet higher than the dirt path they'd left below. He looked out from the cliff and saw the grazing hill below the tree line. He looked out as far as he could to take in the spectacular view from up there. It was simply beautiful, and few other words could truly describe it. The farm's valley was wedged into the middle of an extraordinary landscape. He looked up to see where Billie was. She was gone. A bit of loneliness washed over him.

—

Billie's head peeked up over the top of the cliff, where Antoni and Kate were waiting for her. The cat got up and stretched.

"She's here, Kate!" Antoni whispered quietly with excitement and looked toward Billie's path.

Together they approached the ledge where Billie was coming up. Billie still wasn't safe enough to mob with greetings yet, but they were shimmying back and forth with excitement. *This was happening.* Billie took the last necessary step to reach the safe zone, and her friends sprang.

"You made it!" Antoni cried out. "I knew you had it in you, sister!"

"Billie!" Kate yelled out.

"Quiet now, Antoni. Caesar doesn't even know you're up

here," Billie whispered, smiling at the feline. Then she peered over the ledge to where Caesar was waiting patiently down below. "I've got her, Caesar! She's coming down!"

"I think I changed my mind. I wanna go with you, Billie," Kate whispered.

"I know, I know, but someone has to get poor old Caesar back home safely, and you promised me that much, Kate."

"All right, all right. I wasn't *that* serious. I was just *kinda* serious . . . even though I haven't trained for it and have no business going with you!"

"I think you could do it. You got up here without lifting a hoof to train. Imagine how good you'll be when you practice!" Billie encouraged the friend that made this all possible.

"Maybe next time, Billie Someday," Kate said.

Kate headed back down the cliff face with an ease that made Billie smile. Billie always knew farm goats were capable of more than producing kids and milk. She took a few more steps down the cliff, and before Kate knew it, she was back down near Caesar.

"Kate!" Caesar cried with relief. "Mate, I thought you were gone!"

"I'm fine. I was just helping Billie," Kate said as she came down the last little slope.

Caesar rubbed heads affectionately with Kate when she finally reached his ledge. She'd always been his favorite. When he was done, he looked up to see Billie standing still. She wasn't coming down.

"Helping Billie with what?" Caesar asked as if muzzled.

"I'm gonna climb the Matterhorn, Caesar. We had to do this. I'm sorry we tricked you, mate," Billie said to Caesar.

"Whose approval do you have to climb?" Caesar asked helplessly.

"No one's, Caesar," Billie said from above, without a shred of arrogance.

"Aren't you scared?" Caesar asked, looking up with worried eyes.

"Of course I'm scared. But I just want to make it up to the top of the Matterhorn, then come back home. That way I can live on the farm and still be myself," Billie said.

"Then why don't you come on down and head home with us now, mate?" Caesar pleaded. "I'll look after you. I'll make sure you can be yourself. You can race up the hill and do your stunts every day. I'll make sure of it."

"That's not the same thing. I can't be Billie Someday if I don't do this," she said. "You know it deep down, Caesar. Really, think about it. It's all I ever think about, talk about, dream about. I've gotta do this."

"Ah, crikey." His head dropped, but then he looked back up. "All right, go on. Be Billie, mate."

"Thanks, Caesar. I knew it was somewhere in you," Billie said.

"We'll miss ya, kid!" Caesar said.

"Yeah, Billie, we'll miss you. Be safe gettin' to the top!" Kate said.

"You two get going. Mrs. Wolf knows you're headed back that way soon. Best get a head start on her," Billie said.

"Come on, Kate. We should go," Caesar said to his little friend.

Kate and Caesar climbed down the cliff, back to the slithering dirt path. Billie knew she wouldn't see either of them for quite a while. She was quite saddened by the idea but knew she still had a task of her own at hand. She turned toward her friend Antoni and then started to climb up.

"Pssst. Tell them to take a different route home," Antoni whispered to Billie.

"Oh, good point," she whispered back. Then she hollered down to Caesar and Kate, "Hey! Take a new route back to the grazing hill, you two! It'll be safer!" Billie shouted her advice from up high on the cliff.

Caesar looked back toward the cliff and whispered to himself, "Thanks, Billie Someday. Safe travels, mate. Come back in one piece, will ya?"

"Let's get going before the wolves come back," Kate said to Caesar, then the two trotted back toward the farm on a newly chosen route.

Chapter 23

"**W**ell, where do we go from here? What shall we do first, Antoni?" Billie asked her companion.

She replied, "Mountain climber, I believe you need to learn how to navigate and learn to navigate fast if you want to make it back home in one piece." Antoni's fur-lined ears were perked, listening for warnings, and her tail moved back and forth slowly, showing that she was alert but not alarmed by anything in particular.

"Navigate?" Billie asked. "That sounds boring."

"You want to be able to find your way home when all of this is over, right?"

"Of course."

"Then learn to navigate." Antoni set her straight. "No one is going to be up there with you, and no one can help you find your way up or down. That's all on you now, Billie." She waited, hoping a question or comment of some kind would come from the little goat, but nothing was said. She continued, "First things first, Billie—we need a baseline."

"What's a baseline?"

"I use baselines all the time when I leave the farm. So, home base is the farm, you follow me?"

Billie nodded.

"After that is your secondary home, so to speak: the grazing hill. Your baseline is what connects you to your secondary home, so if you can find your baseline, it'll lead you to the grazing hill, and from the grazing hill, you know how to get home, right?"

"Okay. Yeah, I can always find my way home from the grazing hill," Billie said.

"The thing is, a baseline is your marker, but it can't be in just one spot. It's a *line* after all, right? So it's usually a long, easy-to-find, impossible-to-miss, straightforward *line*. You find the baseline, and it'll lead you home. That's what matters."

"How do I use the baseline to get home?" Billie asked.

"Could you get home from where you are right now?" Antoni answered with a question of her own.

"Yeah, easy. You can see the grazing hill right there. The farm is just below that." Billie pointed with her eyes.

"Correct, so right now we're on the ridge of a cliff. It's pretty hard to miss, right? Look out over there as far as you can see. Looks like it goes a long way, right? How far do you think the ridge goes?" Antoni asked.

"I have no idea. It doesn't look like it ends," Billie answered.

"Super long lines like this one make for a good baseline, and you want one you can't miss. If you can't miss it, that makes it perfect for navigation. So this is your baseline, Billie. The ridge with the cliff. Don't forget it. Etch it into your mind, because once this line ends, the next line you decide to use should point directly to this one. Add a bunch of lines pointing to one another during your trip, and they'll all lead you back to this baseline: the cliff. If you can do that, you can find the grazing hill, and from there you're golden. Easy enough, right?"

Billie thought about it, then said, "That seems pretty rigid, following all these lines. It sounds like rules."

"Nah, you don't have to follow a line perfectly," the cat replied. "Zigzag wherever you want over it, but just know how to use the line. Keep it in the back of your mind."

"As long as there's no wolves around?" Billie asked.

"Exactly. So what's your game plan if a wolf does come around? You know, like just now or before on the grazing hill last winter?"

"Me? I'm heading for the cliff as quickly as I can and finding a place they can't climb to," Billie said.

"That sounds like a plan," Antoni said.

"What about you?" Billie asked. "How are you gonna get away from the wolves? You know, if they show up?"

"I always fancy the trees. If I can get up in a tree, I can hang out on a branch for days if I have to," Antoni said. "But let's hope I don't have to. I'm good at relaxing, but I'm better off on my feet."

"Well then, quit relaxing and get on your *better feet*, because we need to get going if I'm going to climb this mountain," Billie said through a smirk.

Antoni had her paws tucked comfortably underneath her and out of the way. Normally she would stretch before going anywhere, but this time she got up without hesitation and resumed their crossing of Darkwood Forest. Billie was surprised at being left behind so quickly by her friend. Antoni was the one that always seemed to be procrastinating, but Billie caught up to the cat soon enough.

"So what's the farthest you've been in Darkwood?" Billie asked.

"What's the farthest *you've* been in Darkwood?"

"Right here. This is the farthest I've been."

"Well, me too," Antoni said.

Billie kept hiking without talking. She decided, *We're true explorers then, out here doing something no one on the farm has ever done. This is big. This is big.*

And this was only the beginning. This big hiking journey was about to get far more complicated.

—

The journey was going smoothly for the pair, and thus far, it had only cost some time and a little energy. They both had plenty of that, though the terrain was beginning to get more difficult for the shorter-legged Antoni. She was certainly not overtaxed by leaping from lower ground to the next piece of higher ground, but the duration between these leaps was becoming shorter and shorter the higher they climbed. Fatigue became a factor as the ground became rougher. She had less and less time to recover between leaps, making the hike wear on her more and more as they went. This was not her natural habitat.

The pair eventually found their rhythm hiking the ridge along Darkwood Forest. Billie stayed closer to the cliff in case the wolves appeared, and her friend hugged the tree line for the same reason. Antoni dictated the pace, and Billie adjusted her speed so that she didn't get too far ahead. And this was the way they carried on. With little to say, they just hiked along the ridge, looking for where it might end. Looking ahead, they could see there were no more trees, so they figured they must be somewhere near the end of Darkwood.

Antoni suddenly looked nervously at Billie. "Do you feel that? The ground's shaking."

"Wolves!" Billie yelled out just before she leapt over the edge of the cliff. She instantly found a hoofhold, where she held fast, then she asked her friend, "Did you find a tree, Antoni?"

The cat answered with concern in her voice. "Yeah."

"I can't see you," Billie said from her place down a ways from the top of the cliff.

"I can't see you either, kid," Antoni replied from her branch in the pine tree. "I think I know why the ground was shaking."

"Why was it shaking?" Billie asked.

"There's a herd of mountain goats headed this way. Must be a hundred of them."

"Do you see the wolves?" Billie asked. "I think they saw me before I went over the side."

"Yeah, they're underneath my tree looking right up at me. There's a few of them on the edge looking for you too. Do you see them yet?"

"Oh . . . yeah. I see 'em now. One of 'em locked eyes with me. What should I do?"

"Can you go anywhere?" Antoni asked.

"Yeah, I guess. I can go anywhere but up," Billie said.

"Okay, yeah, probably don't do that. There's a pack of seven wolves up here waiting for us. They look kinda beat up though. Some of them are limping and a bit bloody, but I still wouldn't mess with them. It looks like they've been hunting and went after something a little bit too big. A bear, maybe?"

"A bear couldn't do this to wolves," the alpha wolf spoke up. "Merlin got the best of us after we chased that enigma up a slope. This guy here took a fall—he might have broken something. That one there, she got kicked. The others got hit by falling rocks. I got out without getting nicked up, and then Merlin got away. But we'll get him next time."

"Who's Merlin?" Billie asked from the side of the cliff.

"Merlin? That's the ram who got away. That's his name," the alpha said. "He always gets away. We've been chasing him for years, but no one's bested ole Merlin. Ever. He's a magician up on those slopes, but we'll get him one of these days. He'd make minced meat out of you, little goat, so steer clear of him and his lair if you ever make it out of here alive. It looks like your chances of that might have improved."

"Billie!" Antoni said, noticing what the mountain goat herd was doing. "It's about to be our lucky day. Over here! Goats! Over here!"

Billie joined Antoni and started bleating for their attention. "Help! HELP! Over here!"

The mountain goats stopped and looked toward the cries. Their eyes found the wolves, so they encircled the weaker members of the herd. Once their circle became a safe place, the stronger goats moved aggressively toward the wolves.

The wolves spread out in a V formation with the alpha out front. "They've got us outnumbered, pack. Best we move on this time. Anyone that's injured leaves first. I'll follow you after. I'll keep these mountain goats at bay in the meantime. Now go!"

The alpha ran aggressively at the advancing goats, and they stopped their charge. Both the wolf pack and mountain goat herd were cautious of one another. Being banged up, the wolves weren't ready to hunt big game, and the mountain goats knew you could never let your guard down around even a single wolf. The alpha wolf looked back, away from the mountain goats; he noticed his pack had gotten away safely, so he began his own escape, trotting down the cliff's ridgeline.

"I guess it *is* your lucky day, little goat," the alpha wolf said to Billie as he trotted by her on her ledge partway down the cliff. "You found some big friends who like to fight. They might accept you, even though you're a runt, but that cat friend of yours is out of luck. These ones only trust folks with hooves." The alpha looked up at Antoni in the tree. "Why don't you join us, cat? We'd love to have you for dinner."

"Why don't you stay a while, wolf? I bet the taste of four hundred hooves is a meal to die for." Antoni laughed.

"All right, you strange pair of prey, good luck with whatever you're doing up here."

Billie took a breath, stood up as tall as she could, and puffed out her chest. "I'm gonna climb to the top of this mountain, and when I get there, the whole world will know who I am: Billie Someday, the greatest of all time! I even bet this Merlin of yours hasn't been to the *top*!"

"They say Merlin protects the top," the wolf said, "and if you wanna summit the Matterhorn, you'll have to do something I've never done, which is get the best of ole Merlin. He protects the top from fools like you, so good luck with all that. You'll need it."

"I don't need luck! The greatest never needs luck!" Billie yelled at the retreating wolf.

"You're right about that, kid. The greatest doesn't need luck. The greatest makes their own," the alpha replied over his shoulder.

"Get out of here!" The mountain goats charged forward once again. "Get out of here, wolf!"

The wolf trotted away without fear of the mountain goats. He was, after all, the true alpha out there, but maybe just not *the best* on the mountain.

"Is it safe, Antoni?" Billie yelled out.

"Depends. How safe do you feel around giant mountain goats?" Antoni asked.

"Do they eat farm goats?" Billie asked.

"They eat the plants the mountain provides . . . and sometimes they lick salt off the rocks, but we never eat the flesh of another," a young female mountain goat answered out of turn. She was looking down at Billie when she answered. This was the first time Billie had ever seen a mountain goat.

"If that's all they eat, then I can feel safe, being around them," Billie said.

"Then come on up," the young mountain goat said. Billie climbed up to where the herd was. "Do you have hooves?"

"Yep! I've got four," Billie said.

"Then you're all right with me. Let me see what King Goat says." She trotted off.

Billie climbed back to the top of the ridgeline and mingled with the herd she could only hear before. She noticed the females were enormous, with beautiful horns that curved back a little like her own but on a larger scale. The males were even bigger than them, and they had incredibly intimidating thick, knotty horns that twisted back and away from their heads.

"We can't take her," one of the youngest males said. "She's too small. She can't climb like us."

"You can't even climb like us, runt," the fierce King Goat said to that youthful male while charging toward him.

The young male lowered his eyes and found a place in the back of the crowd. The hierarchy of these mountain goats had been established long ago, and the King Goat's word was the last one.

"Farm goat, get over here. Let me look at you. Do you have split hooves or solid ones?" King Goat asked.

"They're split . . . like yours." Billie showed the King her hoof.

"Good, good. Split hooves are good for climbing. Let me see? How shall I test you?" The King looked around. "That boulder there. Climb it."

"I just came up that cliff face a second ago," Billie said.

"Just do it," the young female mountain goat said quietly with her head down.

"She doesn't have to prove anything. She's here. That proves plenty. She can be one of us," an elder doe said.

"Fine," King Goat burst out with frustration in his voice. "You can climb if you want to, but you leave your friend behind, because cats don't climb, and if you don't climb, you ain't no friend of mine."

"I climbed up this tree. Let's see you try that," Antoni quipped but only to herself.

A feminine voice spoke up. It was the elder doe again. "Don't go with them, little farm goat. You can hike around with us. Besides, courtship season is over, and those bachelor bucks will run off after this anyway. The King is just the king of the bachelor herd. We females do our own thing most of the year, but the King is right. Your cat friend won't make it where we're going—you'd do well to follow my herd. It'll be safer with us than with her."

Billie looked up into the tree where Antoni was still perched. Antoni said, "Billie, I was never gonna be able to go all the way. You and I, we're built differently, you know. You have a gift, kid— go use it."

"What will you do from here?" Billie asked her feline friend.

Antoni replied, "I'll follow the ridge down and head back to the farm."

"Are you sure you'll be okay?"

"I always have the trees. I'm more worried about you. Do you know where you're going next?" Antoni asked Billie about her plans.

The elder doe spoke out of turn. "This mountain's our home. We know where we're going, and we'll take her with us."

"I meant for her. She's got goals you won't understand, highborn," Antoni said to the leader of Billie's new herd.

"What's that supposed to mean?" the elder mountain goat asked.

"She's different from you, and she has different goals, too. The sooner you figure that out, the better off she'll be," Antoni said. "She's not trying to be one of you."

"It's fine, Antoni. I can figure this out. Maybe this will end up being the best way to get up the mountain," Billie said.

"Up, up, up, then down, down, down. That's how mountain goats get around," the young female mountain goat said.

Antoni said, "All right, I'm coming down from this branch. Don't stomp me."

"I won't let them," Billie said fiercely as the cat made its way down.

Antoni said, "I'm not exactly hungry like the wolf, but I'm getting hungry like the cat, if you all know what I'm saying. Do any of you know if there are mice around here?"

"No, I don't, but I can assure you that no one here will harm you if you want to hunt for mice. You have my word." The King Goat turned to Billie. "Say your goodbyes, our new little mountain goat. We should all get going our separate ways."

"She's not a mountain goat," Antoni whispered so only Billie could hear her.

Billie waited until the herd gave her and Antoni some space to talk alone. "When you leave, my last connection to the farm is gone."

"When I leave, *you* are your last connection to the farm. Don't forget that you're a mountain-*climbing* goat, not a mountain goat. Don't lose yourself, Billie," Antoni said solemnly.

"I won't. I've never forgotten who I am."

"Not your identity, Billie. I mean don't lose your life. I'd miss you too much."

"I won't."

"Before we escaped, Sappho told me to tell you she loves you. And you know your mother loves you too, right?"

"I know." Billie kept her eyes down.

Antoni sat quietly for a moment. "And I love you, Billie."

"I love you too, Antoni." Their eyes were fixed on each other.

"I believe in you, kid. Whatever comes of this, you . . . you're amazing, Billie Someday."

"Thanks. And thanks for coming all this way. I wouldn't be right here if it weren't for you."

"I know. Be safe, kid."

"I will."

Antoni turned and started back down the ridge with her pilose tail in the air, waving it gently as only a cat can do. Billie watched her get farther and farther away without looking anywhere else. She felt her eyes tearing up, so she looked toward the herd of mountain goats, then looked back for Antoni. Antoni had disappeared, just like that. Billie couldn't control the flood of tears any longer. She turned toward the herd. The elder doe saw Billie first and decided to approach her.

"Sorry," Billie said, her voice choked up. She was embarrassed by her own tears.

"Don't be sorry. There's strength in emotion. It's the truest strength of a bond."

Chapter 24

"**U**se your speed, does! We've gotta make Hex Pasture before sundown," the elder doe cried out to her herd. "Dooooeeeesss, readyyyy!?"

"Ready!" the does answered her call.

"Go! Go! Go!" said the elder.

Billie was not expecting any herd to follow commands from a leader within. She was used to Caesar dishing out this kind of motivation, or the farmer, or maybe someone using trickery to move their crowds back home. Now there was this comrade—one of them—leading the way. Before she knew it, the mountain goats were off to the races, and Billie was the last member in a line of this new herd. Her herd. She was now an honorary member of the ibex, and the slowest one in the group at that. Billie was the smallest, had the shortest legs, and now was the slowest. Even the eldest ibex moved through these slopes like a crow flying through the air. It looked effortless for them. This pace wasn't making Billie too tired necessarily, but the route was much too jagged and unstable for her to maintain the fast pace they kept. To her, it felt dangerous.

"You'll get used to the speed!" the youngest female shouted back to Billie when she saw her struggling.

Billie was breathing heavily. "When?" she shouted.

"Before you know it!" the youngest female shouted back again.

That's not a real answer, Billie thought. *That's not even helpful.*

"What's your name? I didn't hear you say it before," Billie asked.

The young female stopped and turned. As Billie caught up, she said, "I'm Teena—nice to meet you. It's Billie, right?"

"Yep. So what's the trick for going so fast?"

Teena started trotting and suddenly took off, in a full gallop Billie couldn't imagine performing herself. "Jump around! Go ahead and jump! Jump! Might as well jump around! Jump! Jump! Jump!"

My goodness, she's talented, but this isn't helpful at all, Billie thought. After watching for a moment, Billie decided to give this "jump, jump, jump" strategy a try. *I must look pretty goofy,* she thought to herself, but then decided, *When in a herd on the Matterhorn, jump as the Matterhorn goats do.*

Billie took to this bouncing around with some practice, enough to keep pace with the new herd, but it still felt unsafe going this fast. Simply put, she was overdoing it. As she went on and on in this jumping fashion, she thought to herself, *What in the world are you doing, Billie Someday? You're about to fly off the mountain following these ibex. They're not even going up the Matterhorn! They're going across it! What's the point?*

Just as Billie allowed negative thoughts to consume her, she landed on a patch of soft ground that couldn't hold firm under her weight. She lost her grip on the path and started to slide with the loose rocky footing, over the side. Billie Someday was in trouble.

"Teena! Help!" Billie cried out, clinging to a single hoofhold desperately.

"Billie! Where are you?" Teena yelled out, retracing her jumps.

"Over here!" Billie yelled back.

Teena spotted her hanging there. "You can do this!"

"I'm gonna fall!" Billie said.

"I know. I'm saying you can fall."

"I'll die though."

"No, you can fall fine here if you want."

"I don't wanna fall!"

"Can you climb up?"

"No."

"Then you're gonna have to fall."

"What?"

"Failure's a great teacher. You'll see. Just fall the best that you can."

"How do I fall 'best'?"

"Push off, and let yourself fall hooves-first. Then they'll find something to slow you down. Just trust your hooves. It's easy."

Billie remembered the leaps she made as a kid off the red dirt pile, but the red dirt was a much softer landing than this jagged slope. "I don't wanna do it."

"Fine! Watch me first," Teena said as she plunged over the top of Billie's head and down the steep mountain, going headfirst.

If Billie thought Teena was fast traversing the mountain paths, going straight down its slope she looked like a falcon diving after its prey. Billie's heart raced, knowing that this kind of speed going straight down the mountain would be deadly for her. But Teena's hooves found something, and she took a stride that only slightly altered her downward momentum. Then she took another and turned a little more to the right. *She's gonna make it,* Billie thought. Two more strides, and Teena converted a freefall into a gentle landing like a bird, bending away from the earth, and away, and away, until it was safe to stop.

Her new friend gave her the confidence to go for it. "Here I go!"

Billie dropped like a stone, and her heart raced. Everything happened quickly. She couldn't feel the air moving by her, she couldn't feel her racing heart, and she couldn't feel her fear trying to penetrate her thoughts. She could only concentrate on her hooves as she braced for contact. *Wham!* The impact of the slopes hurt her joints, but it didn't matter—she needed to use the impact to slow herself down. The first stride allowed her to turn a little, and the next a little more. But then her front hooves buckled, her ankle popped, and she rolled to a painful stop. Billie grimaced as Teena approached.

"Almost!" Teena was encouraging.

"I think I broke something." Billie was in pain.

"You're bleeding some, but I've seen worse," said Teena.

"Ugh. Where?"

"Right there." Teena motioned at Billie's shoulder. "It'll be okay. Can you walk?"

"I don't know. My knee got banged up."

"Well, if you lie there, it's probably not gonna work out so well."

"Why not?"

"Bears come up here sometimes."

"Okay, okay. I get it. I'll get up," Billie said as she struggled to get to her feet.

"It's simple up here, Billie Someday," Teena said. "Life goes on or it doesn't."

"Gotcha." She paused. "I guess I'll try to walk."

Billie took a few steps to shake it off. Her freshly earned limp slowed her down, but at least she was mobile.

"We fell behind with that little detour. We need to get over to Hex Pasture if we're gonna sleep safely. How fast can you move?"

"I can keep going, but I can't go as fast as you were going before. You go ahead. I'll figure something out."

"We'll be fine. We're gonna get there, but it might be a while."
Teena began to move forward, and Billie followed. "So do you
know any stories? Ibex love stories."

"That's not really my thing, but my grandma knows quite a
few," Billie said. "I just listen to stories. Do you know any?"

"Of course! All ibex love stories! What do you want to hear?"

"Tell me one about Merlin the Magician!" Billie said somewhat enthusiastically, considering the pain she was in.

"Oh, so you know about him down in the valley?"

"Yeah, sort of, but not from down in the valley. The wolves
told me about him."

"Hmm. Well, they say he was never born but just appeared one
day in the fog, and he's been the top ram ever since. Before his
reign, mountain goats made annual pilgrimages to the top of the
Matterhorn, but Merlin doesn't let anyone touch the top anymore.
Everyone who challenges him—ram, ibex, bear, or wolf—they
all go flying down the mountain when he thumps them with his
horns. He's so big that you'd rather try to move a boulder than
move Merlin. He can change the direction of the wind with a
swing of his horns. Even the mountain itself is afraid of Merlin,
and you can feel it shudder sometimes in fear. He has this whole
region under his spell, but as long as you leave him alone, he'll
leave you alone. However, if you challenge him, get ready to
breathe your last breath—he'll trample you as easily as you trample a blade of grass."

Billie looked down at a blade of grass in front of her and
smashed it. She took her hoof off the blade. Indeed it was trampled, but it only bent—it wasn't broken. She watched it slowly rise
again in defiance.

"Has he ever been challenged?"

"The wolves challenge him every year, and every year they

limp back to their den. One time, King Goat went to the High Crest of the Matterhorn to challenge Merlin, and the King's knees buckled before Merlin even touched him. He's unbeatable."

"Maybe for you," Billie said.

"Maybe for me? What could you do? You're half my size, maybe less," Teena said.

"Size isn't everything."

"He's not just big. He's fast, powerful, and smart as a fox."

"How big is his heart?" Billie asked.

"What do you mean?" Teena asked.

"Don't worry about it," Billie said. "Let's just get where we're going and catch some sleep."

—

"Last to camp gets the last bed, stragglers," the elder doe declared as Billie and Teena approached the Hex Pasture, where the ibex does were already lying in the places they'd found to sleep.

All the good spots were taken, so Billie and Teena bedded down on the inclined pathway between two boulders. Their shared spot wasn't flat enough to lie on properly, but they were both so exhausted they slept like babies.

"Rise and shine, goats!" the elder cried out at daybreak.

It didn't feel, to Billie, as if she had slept long enough, but the herd was moving on.

"We're heading down to Penta Pasture this morning. We need water and salt," the elder doe said.

"Down? I need to go up," Billie said, loudly enough that the elder doe heard her.

"There's an easy way up when you go down. You go over, then across and down again. After that, you can go up. We'll go then . . . if I say so."

"I'm trying to get to the top of this mountain, not across it or down it! Up it! Up to the top before the snow starts creeping in!" Billie said in frustration.

"If you're one of us, you'll do what we do, no questions asked. When you're up this high, you have to do what everyone else does, or you won't last with us," the elder said to Billie.

Billie looked Teena in the eye and calmly said to all who were listening, "I'm not one of you. I'm Billie, a farm goat from the valley, and I'm climbing the Matterhorn all the way to the top."

The elder paused in thought, then said, "We need water and salt. There's neither if you go up. So we go down. Merlin the Magician is the Protector of the Peak—we respect all he stands for, so we don't go near the top. We don't challenge his authority. We don't even go near High Crest unless it's to pay respect. Trying to go to the summit would be pure disrespect. What right do you think you have to disrespect Merlin, Billie Someday?" she asked, disgust in her tone.

"I'm a mountain-climbing farm goat." Billie hesitated, knowing what she needed to do next. "I'm leaving your herd. I'll find my own way from here. Greatness waits for me somewhere up *above* High Crest . . . *above* this Merlin character."

The elder doe said, "This is all above your head, little one. You have no idea what you're up against. If you're smart, you'll go home and let this dream of yours die."

"If you knew as much as you think you know, you'd know words never stop me," Billie said.

Chapter 25

Getting as far as she had on this journey, Billie was sure of one thing. The path the mountain goats chose wasn't for her. And she knew how to climb and how to navigate already. The ibex didn't teach her much at all about climbing. Antoni taught her how to follow the lines on her way up to the Matterhorn, and those lines would help her return home once she was on top of it all. She just needed to get back to the last line she'd drawn in her mind before she joined the ibex, that ridge she had drawn in her mind when climbing up it with Antoni earlier. She was confident she could navigate if she could get back to that path. She believed in her climbing ability, in her ways and her ideas, but she didn't have that same faith in the mountain goats' ways. It might work for them, but she needed to do it the Billie Someday way. Besides, the path the elder doe picked out for the herd made Billie feel lost. So she left them behind and limped along the route that she picked out for herself. The path that led back to Antoni's ridge. Her baseline. Soon enough, she'd reset her route and be climbing toward the summit of the Matterhorn again.

Billie walked away from the ibex herd using the same path they used to get to Hex Pasture. Teena trotted up behind her as she was leaving. "Wait, Billie!" she cried. "Please don't leave. We can help you. There's a way up to the High Crest just around the next bend. Don't give up!"

"I'm not giving up. I'm doing this my way." Billie was aggravated by her wasted attempt to become one of the ibex.

"Yes, you are, but you're not going the right way," Teena replied.

"You can't possibly believe that everything done your herd's way is the right way, can you?"

"I mean . . . no, but we do know a really good route. This is our home, so of course we know the best ways to get around it."

"You know *your* ways around the Matterhorn that work for you, but you don't know my way because you've never tried it. You're fast because you were born fast—you've never been forced to go slow. You can fall with grace because you were born to fall with grace. You live up high because you were born this high, and you know the way around mountain paths because you follow what everyone else around you does on the mountain. You never make your own path. I'm not like that. I worked my whole life making my own path to get here, to this place you were born. You're too rooted in your way of life to see what I'm doing," Billie said. "I'm making this happen."

"How do you plan to do it?" Teena asked.

"I'll figure it out."

"How will you figure it out?"

Billie was annoyed by the lack of faith. "I can't always figure it out at first, Teena, but I've kept going and going until I've found a way. There're no tricks, no magical appearances where I'm suddenly where I want to be through a fog. It's just me with this body and brain I was born with."

"This is foolish, Billie. How are you doing this alone?"

"What's foolish is you being born free to climb, yet you've never even tried to get to the top of the mountain."

"It's not like that. It's more dangerous than you think. Danger is all around here, even if you don't see it," said Teena.

"It is dangerous, but *that* doesn't stop me."

"It's too risky," Teena said.

"I'm willing to take those risks even if you're not. And I'll take them on my own if I have to."

"You've never even seen Merlin. How do you plan to get past *him?*"

"I have seen him . . . from far away, but I know I'll get past him if I do it my way."

Teena watched Billie limp away, fierce and determined. Billie never looked back, but both she and Teena wished they'd parted on a better hoof. They were both too critical of one another, and because of this, they had never found the common ground they desired. Even though the new herd didn't work out for her, Billie was still thankful for the herd scaring off the wolves. Teena was coming around to the idea that she should be thankful for learning something new about herself and her herd from Billie Someday. Billie gave Teena another view of the world she'd always known. Teena thought to herself, *Maybe by following the elder doe's every command all the time, I end up missing out on some things in life? Maybe I can do my own thing sometimes, too. Maybe.*

—

Billie returned to the ridge where she last saw Antoni. She looked for the wolves. She had seen the wolves at this very location earlier in her journey, so there was nothing to stop them from being there now, but Billie convinced herself to stay calm. They had no reason to be there now, and when she looked around, she saw there were none.

"One line leads to the next, Billie. Where's the next line?

Where is it?" Billie said to herself out loud while looking around. "There . . . that'll be the next one!"

This will work, she thought. *It goes up, over, and points toward the peak. That's perfect.*

Billie was happy to be making her own decisions again. *This feels right*, she thought to herself as she looked up at a new line off of the exposed ridge she was on. *It's pretty windy going up here, but this way'll get me where I'm going. It has to.*

Billie had been climbing for a while, and now the sun was making its daily decision to go down for the night, so Billie thought she'd do the same. She found a place in the dirt that blocked the wind, and she settled herself down in it. She felt tired lying there curled up on the rocky ground of the Matterhorn, but at least her knee and shoulder felt better than they did when she woke up next to Teena earlier that morning. She watched a snowflake gently zigzag through the air and fall in front of her hoof.

"Oh, great," Billie said, remembering that up in the high altitudes, it got cold enough to snow . . . even during the summer.

—

Billie rose from her slumber and shook off the snowflakes that had collected on her overnight. It wasn't a lot of snow, but it reminded her that this window of opportunity to climb wouldn't last forever. She put her head down and her rump up and got moving.

Not too long after she woke up, the sun had almost reached a midpoint in the sky and melted the snow that lay on the ground around her. Looking up, she saw snow packed to the side of the peak. She knew she might have to contend with that snow later, but today she wouldn't have any around her to worry about, so she put her head back down and focused on the steps right in front of her.

With her head down, Billie didn't notice the golden eagle with its eye on her from up in the sky. She also couldn't see Teena way above her kicking rocks toward her, but she heard the effects of it because the rocks slid down on either side of her. She looked up and spotted her. *There's the culprit . . . Teena!*

"That jealous rascal," Billie said to herself. Then she yelled out, "Hey, you! Teena! Stop that!"

Teena was moving her head wildly back and forth, but Billie couldn't hear what she was saying. Teena was just too far away to be heard.

Billie was hit by a rock. "Ow!" she cried out, running up the hill to avoid more collisions. As she ran up, she found a tiny little protected cave. She decided to duck into it to ride the landslide out. As she turned into the opening of the cave, a golden blur swooped in close by.

Whoosh. Whoosh. Whoosh.

Billie reached her head out to see where the whoosh came from. As she poked her neck out, the golden blur swooped down again, talons out, and tried to pick her up.

Krrrrr. WHAM. Eeeek! Skraaa. WHOOSH. WHOOsh. Whoosh.

The cacophony of sounds evaporated slowly until the wind was the only noise Billie could hear. It sounded safe again, so she poked her head out once more.

"Hey!" the familiar voice squealed as Billie looked for it. "Up here." Teena was up on top of the little cave, looking down beneath her hooves at the little farm goat. She was staring at Billie. Teena came down the slope to join Billie while she was tucked into her rock shelter.

"What are you doing here?" Billie asked, still unsure of the young mountain goat's intentions.

"I thought you were a goner!"

"What do you mean?" Billie asked suspiciously.

"That eagle was after you, dude! It was so close. I warned you the best way I could, but then you found the cave!"

"How'd you know about the cave?"

"I used to hang out in there when I was little. I'm too big for the eagles now, but you're not. This cave is still the perfect size for you, though." Billie was still confused. "Come on! Let's go up to the High Crest. They won't mess with you if I'm with you. The rams will, but I mean the eagles . . . the eagles won't mess with you. The rams are probably a different story."

"Thanks, I guess?" Billie said, but then thought better of her phrasing. "Wait, no . . . I don't guess. This is just a plain old humble thank-you. I owe you one."

"Don't mention it. You do what you do, and I do what I do. Doesn't mean we can't help each other out."

"True." Billie was happy to have the company.

"I think we can help each other out pretty well going forward from here," Teena said.

"You're pretty good at helping me, but how can I help you?"

"Well, you're gonna go take on Merlin. If you best him, then you get to make the new rules for the Matterhorn, if you decide to make them. That's the way it works—if you best him, you're in charge, and I've always wanted to see the world from the peak of the Matterhorn, like my ancestors used to before Merlin banned everyone from going to the top. I want you to beat Merlin so you can change the rules—change them so the rams have to let us go back to the summit."

"I'm not really trying to rule over anything, but that's a deal. I'll change the laws of the Matterhorn if I best Merlin. I'll make it so that anyone can try for the top if they're good enough to make it there." Billie paused. "But why are you here? Where's the rest of your herd?"

Teena replied, "I left them. The elder doe took the mountain goats down for salt, and I just kind of went up when no one was paying attention. I told you we know the mountain—I knew I'd run into you when I went my way. The route that I knew made it easy, too."

"But why are you here with me? I thought you believed in your ways, following the leader and all that."

"Remember what you said to me? That I was foolish not to at least try to make it to the top? I think I miss out by doing what everyone else is doing. What you're doing, no one else is even trying, and I wanna help."

"Have you been to the High Crest where this Merlin reigns?"

"Yeah, of course. We go once a year to pay our respects to the Magician of the Mountain."

"How much farther is it?"

"About half a day's climb. Maybe a little more."

"At your pace or mine?" Billie asked.

"At our pace . . . and it's about half a day at that rate."

Billie grinned at the idea of *our pace*.

"There's another cave up ahead. It's bigger than that one you're sittin' in. That's where we need to aim. We can sleep there tonight, and if I'm right, we can use it to get you close to Merlin tomorrow, unimpeded by the other rams guarding the path to High Crest."

"Teena, I wasn't sure I wanted it earlier, but thanks for the help. I'm glad you're here."

—

It was morning now. The farm goat and ibex pair had made it to the cave the night before and rested all night within the rocky shelter. Billie was feeling refreshed. This day had great potential, and the world just outside the cave seemed to know it too, because it was bustling gloriously with morning life. Teena poked her head out to look for the enemy's position. "It looks like they're still up there. They're in the same places they were last night."

"All of them?" Billie replied.

"Yeah, I think so. I'll have to go into the canyon to know for sure, but there might be more now," Teena said as she walked up toward the canyon's valley floor.

The canyon wasn't far from the cave. It had been an important landmark to both the mountain goats and the rams since the beginning of Merlin's reign. This was because the cave was so close to the entrance of the canyon, and the entrance was not a difficult hike from the cave. It made the cave a good resting place for ibex on the way to pay their yearly respects to Merlin. The valley of the canyon formed the only path that could get you to High Crest, and that's where Merlin made his home. This meant that the rams could protect the canyon to prevent intruders from getting to Merlin unannounced. That is, unless you were Billie Someday.

The rams guarding the canyon saw Billie and Teena enter the cave the night before, but let them rest peacefully all night. If mountain goats minded their manners, obeyed the rules of the mountain, and followed directions when they entered the canyon, all was well. If they did not, there'd be consequences for the mountain goats. Teena returned to the cave. "Billie, I really think this is gonna work."

"So they're all protecting the canyon?"

"Yep. As far as I can tell. We must've really alarmed them last night. They're lining every ridge. They're spread all across the canyon."

"Well, good luck with your part," Billie said.

Teena replied, "And good luck with yours too."

"I won't need it," Billie said, smirking.

"Sometimes it's better to be lucky than good, Billie Someday, but either way, if you do this, I'll be grateful forever. All mountain goats will be, if you can pull this off."

Teena nodded, then marched back into the canyon alone. The rams were perched on the canyon walls, as they always were when Merlin was staying on the High Crest. They watched everything she did from up where they were. They had seen this mountain goat enter the resting cave the night before with a little farm goat, and they were suspicious of the pair. Teena knew her herd wasn't supposed to pay respects until later that year, but here she was, marching through the protected canyon unannounced and at the wrong time of the year.

"Halt!" Merlin's guardian shouted.

Teena looked up at the guardian, who sat high above her atop the canyon walls. He was huge and intimidating. However, she ignored his command and kept marching.

"Halt in the name of Merlin the Magician, first of his name and true king of the mountain!" Merlin's guardian shouted again.

Teena looked up at the guardian but continued her march undeterred. Frustrated by Teena's advance, the ram who had just ordered her to halt charged down the wall. His movement toward the young ibex in the valley of the canyon was made with great impunity. Three more guardians did the same afterward. They were all completely unconcerned with any backlash from their aggressive actions, but even with the display of physical intimidation, she kept marching. The four guardians lined up shoulder to shoulder and then attempted to create a blockade, but the fearless mountain goat went around them peacefully. She did so without touching them, and the guardians didn't touch her either. Touching any mountain goat was forbidden by their peace treaty, but an ibex entering High Crest without Merlin's blessing was forbidden as well. This created a dilemma for the rams.

"This is in direct violation of our peace treaty. If you do not stop, we will stop you," the guardian shouted into Teena's face, but Teena just kept marching.

"Round up, guardians! All rams! Full circle!" Merlin's lead guard shouted.

Merlin's entire guard charged down the canyon walls and surrounded the lone mountain goat. When Teena could see that all the guardian rams were there, she halted. She turned and counted them.

"Finally," Teena said. "Is that all of you?"

"We ask the questions, mountain goat. Now, where's your friend, and what are you doing here at the beginning of the summer?" the guardian asked. "Ibex pay their respects at the beginning of fall."

"What am I doing here? Helping. And where is my friend, you ask? She's challenging Merlin. She's taking on the Magician of the Mountain as we speak."

"Impossible. We've had this canyon monitored all night and all morning."

"Are you sure this is the only way up to High Crest?" Teena asked.

Chapter 26

"MERLINNNNN!!!" Billie paused and waited for the echoes to pass. "I, BILLIE SOMEDAY, CHALLENGE YOU!"

"I've seen you before, haven't I, Billie Someday?" Merlin said from somewhere in the shadows. "Have you brought the farmer and the power of his gun with you today?"

"I'm alone. Come out and face me," Billie said.

"That's a shame. The farmer was your only chance of walking away from this unharmed," he said.

"Don't worry about me. Worry about yourself," she quickly replied.

"I don't think you've grown since the last time I saw you, little one."

"Looks can be deceiving. I'm stronger than ever."

"Your eyes are the same as they were that day, fierce, but you clearly don't know what you're up against."

"If you're as great as they say, why do you stall?" Billie asked. "Face me!"

"I didn't permit you to be here. How did you get past my guards?"

"Through the back of the cave where your guardians let us

rest. It has tunnels too small for great big rams like yourselves. It's too small for most, too small for you to notice. For me, though, those little tunnels were exactly what I needed to get here."

SSCLACK. CLACK. Clack. Clack.

Merlin waited for the echo of his hooves hitting the rock to fade. "Even if you did beat me, what would you do with the prize? You're not ready to handle the prize, much less capable of handling it."

"You don't need to know what I'll do. You need to know that this is a challenge. If you don't accept, your reign is over. That's how it works, does it not?"

Merlin scaled a boulder that had blocked Billie's view of him before. "You have no witness?"

"You're my witness. If you have any honor, you'll tell everyone what happened here today when it's all over. You'll tell them the truth. All of them," Billie said.

SSCLACK . . . CLACK . . . Clack . . . clack.

Billie didn't wait for the echoes to stop. "I CHALLENGE YOU, MERLIN!"

Merlin hopped down from his perch in the shadows with ease and met Billie on level ground. He let out a low rumble.

Hhrrooooorrrhhh.

Fog billowed from the great magician's nostrils as he stared Billie down. He scraped at a spot in the dirt to give his enormous hooves a place to launch from. Billie did the same with her front hooves. She looked down and saw a buttercup flower beneath her hoof that she'd been scraping at. It reminded her of the little grazing hill down in the valley and her little farm that she had come from. Merlin noticed that she'd lost her focus on him when she looked down, so he launched his attack.

On his two hind legs, he went up, his torso high in the air and his two front legs pulled into his chest. His huge, spiraled horns were now positioned for battle, but she didn't know if he'd try to trample her with his hooves or attack with his horns. All she knew was that he was about to strike with either one of those and, from the looks of it, strike with a force she'd never even imagined having to absorb. Billie moved forward and lowered her own head while keeping her eyes peeled for how Merlin's attack might land. He was charging at Billie with his horns, and she tried to dodge the blow, but it was too late. Merlin had come down hard on the side of Billie's own little horns and sent her flying. She deflected off his charge and spun away in a cloud of dust, rocks, and pain.

Hhrrooooooorrrrrhhh.

This charge took nothing out of the ram. He was still composed while Billie had taken the hardest shot she'd ever felt. Calmly, she composed herself and rose from her tumble. "Give up yet?" she asked.

Merlin let out a hearty laugh while Billie moved sideways and repositioned herself. "Admitting defeat may not be in your nature, farm goat, but it's about to be."

Merlin reared back up on his two hind legs, front legs out, then he pulled them in and charged again. Billie dug out a launching place in the dirt, anticipating his second assault. Before he lowered his horns to ram Billie again, she charged. She slipped underneath Merlin's front hooves without being touched and scraped the Magician's belly with her horns, going past him safely under his attack.

"Are you trying to win a tickle fight, little Billie?"

Billie didn't reply; she just repositioned herself for the next charge. He did the same. Again he went up on two hind legs with intentions to drive his opponent from the battlefield. Billie avoided the blow again and went underneath Merlin, scraping his underside yet again, a little harder this time.

"Admit it, Merlin," she cried. "That one got you."

"Take me head-on, coward," Merlin said as he hastily positioned himself for another charge. Billie reacted quickly as well, and this time she got the angle she needed.

Once again, Merlin couldn't get his legs down before Billie was underneath him. She aimed her attack at his back right leg, and she hit it with all her might. Merlin the Magician of the Matterhorn, the great ram who reigned over every slope on this mountain, the ruler with no equal, lost his footing . . . *and went down.*

Filled with rage over being embarrassed, Merlin charged at Billie without rearing up on his hind legs. He simply lowered his head and charged on all four hooves. Billie was too late to parry, so she dove out of the way of Merlin's charge. He got a piece of her hind legs, and she was sent tumbling again. But this time, a boulder stopped her momentum.

The guardian rams arrived at the scene on High Crest, where the battle would continue on for them to witness. Because this was an "honorable battle" in their eyes, they were not allowed to interfere in the challenge, only watch. Both participants were dusted up already, and their legs appeared to be growing tired. Billie looked over at the audience from the sinister spot where she'd been tossed into the base of the boulder. She spotted Teena among them. Staring at her friend, she rose from the middle of a cloud of dust that was settling around her. Little spheres of breath billowed from Billie's nostrils. She looked around at her battlefield and noticed a ledge she could quickly hop to. *Perfect.*

Merlin noticed Billie's focus was on something else and sped toward her with his attack on all four legs once again. Billie locked eyes with him. As he sped up and got closer, he lowered his enormous, spiraled horns and aimed straight for her head. He clenched his teeth and closed his eyes, waiting for the impact with Billie. In a split second, Billie jumped to the ledge, then onto Merlin's back. Merlin lifted his head, looking for his missed target, but it was too late. He had charged straight into the boulder beneath Billie's ledge, knocking himself out. Billie fell off of the back of her opponent during the impact between magician and boulder. The mighty buck fell to the ground in a heap. The audience was shocked. Even the wind on the Matterhorn fell silent.

"We won!" Teena screeched, seeing Merlin go down. "Billie! You did it!"

Billie was dazed by the blows she endured in the battle she just fought, but she still had every bit the look of a champion.

"Billie!" Teena yelled as she approached her.

Billie was all smiles. "I'm not done yet."

The audience was still shocked by what they had witnessed. They watched silently as Billie Someday limped along slowly, one hoof in front of the other. She went across the High Crest of the mountain toward a little path that could lead her to an even higher place. The little path Billie found was the way up to the summit of the Matterhorn. With each step toward the summit, she felt stronger inside. Bruised, scraped up, and even limping, she felt stronger than she'd ever felt before.

"BILLIE SOMEDAY!" his voice echoed. "You didn't beat me! You have yet to take me head-on." Merlin had gotten up from his knockdown. He yelled at his opponent, who was headed toward the peak, looking to stop her. "You have no right to summit the Matterhorn—it's still my mountain."

Billie looked back down at the mighty Merlin below her. Even after all that damage he took, he still looked formidable. From her spot well above him, he still looked too big to be beaten head-on.

"Face me! This challenge isn't over!" Merlin continued yelling up at her.

Billie looked down at the audience of rams below her. She knew the guardians could chase her up the mountain and knock her off the trail at any point if just one of them wanted to do it. She came all this way; she fought Merlin and knocked him down twice. *Why isn't that enough?* she thought.

Teena looked up at her friend calmly. She stared and waited until Billie's eyes found hers. Billie saw her friend's lips try to tell her something. "Fall," she said. "Fall, Billie."

Billie couldn't make out what she was trying to say.

"Fall, Billie, fall."

"Fall?" Billie said, looking down at the mighty Merlin.

Billie had figured out what her friend was encouraging her to do. She didn't want to do it, but she had no choice. Billie raised up on two hind legs and threw herself down the mountain hooves-first. As she was gliding, she lowered her head and found a place to aim her fall. With all of her weight, momentum, downward speed, and might—with every piece of her heart—she charged straight down at the reigning champion's spiraled horns.

SSHCLACK. Clack, clack, clack!

Billie made *solid* head-to-head contact that echoed across the mountain. Merlin's knees buckled, and he wobbled backward. He wobbled until he could no longer stay up and collapsed to the ground next to Billie.

Billie was shaken by the blow she'd delivered, but after a moment, she somehow found the power to stand up. She was steady enough on her hooves to take a few steps forward. She limped for a few more steps over to where the mighty Merlin had fallen, put her front two hooves on top of the shoulder of her opponent, and scanned the entirety of High Crest, locking eyes with each of the guardians. "Can I climb this mountain now?" Angry tears were welling in her eyes as she asked them.

All of the rams in the audience took a knee and lowered their heads. She was in pain from all of the bruises she'd earned on the journey to get here, but Billie limped away toward the little path once again—the path heading toward the summit of the Matterhorn. All of the witnesses watched her limp up the path until she disappeared behind a boulder on the trail. The summit was to be hers that day.

One of Merlin's guardians quietly approached Teena and whispered, "Who was that?"

Teena replied, "That was Billie Someday . . . she's the greatest of all time."

Chapter 27

Billie's head was held high as she marched down the slopes of the Matterhorn. She knew she wasn't quite the same with her new limp. Thus she wasn't overconfident, but she was still relaxed and poised in this moment. She had a thousand-yard stare deep within her gaze, and it could tell you an entire story, *if* you looked closely enough. She followed her trail, marching leisurely on the path that was homeward bound.

She was coming over the top of a crest, and when she got over the peak of it, she looked down the slope that was now in front of her. She just happened to be looking at that one ridge she'd already visited during the journey to the top of the Matterhorn. Billie was seeing this place for the third time—it was where she left Antoni and joined up with the ibex. It also just so happened that on this day, on this trail, the alpha wolf and his pack of seven behind him were waiting for her return.

"We thought you'd come back this way after you failed. Looks like we were right," the alpha wolf said, eyeing the little farm goat, whose limp was still showing. "Looks like you got the bad end of a battle with Merlin too, eh? Well, it matters not. Surely you're ready for our feast, right? Because I can tell ya, Billie Someday, I know we are. We're starving."

Mrs. Wolf, the same wolf she'd met on the cliff with Caesar, spoke up from the pack: "Hello, Billie. Didn't I tell you not to let us catch you here again? It seems you're a slow learner. That's too bad for you."

Billie didn't say a thing. She just continued walking along the path, headed directly toward the wolf pack with a smirk on her face. She was no mountain hare in this real-life story. She was a fearless hero.

"This one's gonna be easy, pack!" the alpha wolf said.

"It's never easy, wolf . . . ," Merlin said, marching over the top of the crest behind Billie. Now both Billie and Merlin were descending on the wolves. "And she didn't fail," Merlin added. "She's the champion of the Matterhorn, and my reign is over. The era of Billie Someday has arrived, and this reign is hers. I suggest you bow your heads and show her the respect she's earned."

Billie turned back and nodded at Merlin for his gracious words. Merlin returned a respectful nod back to the new champion of the Matterhorn. She looked back at the pack of wolves and continued the march toward her home, the farm. The wolves moved forward to surround the pair, then Teena and the guardian rams came over the ridge, and the mountain goats followed them. Billie was leading a diverse herd far too powerful for any pack of wolves.

"Don't even try it, wolf. I promise it won't be worth the effort," Merlin said.

"Little Billie Someday bested you, Magician?" the alpha wolf asked Merlin.

Merlin bowed his head and continued the march down the ridge of the baseline that marked Billie's way home.

"Well, Billie," the alpha said. "What's it like up there at the top?"

"Why don't you go see for yourself? I'm not here to stop you or anyone. That's what it's about, right? Finding out for yourself?"

"All right, Billie. We know a good fight when we see one. This isn't it. Maybe we'll catch you later, when you all split up," the alpha wolf said. "All right, wolf pack! Retreat!"

"See you soon, Billie." Mrs. Wolf said, then followed her pack.

Billie never said another word to the departing wolves. She didn't need to. They knew.

———

Billie led her motley herd all the way to the zigzagging path coming off the grazing hill that eventually led to the farm. She was leading them back to her home. As she got closer and closer, the farm goats watched in amazement from inside the grownup pen, but they weren't the only ones to take notice. Antoni popped out from a grass tunnel a few steps in front of Billie, blocking her way. The gray cat with hair spiking up above her ears stopped in the middle of the path and stared at Billie joyfully with her piercing golden eyes, proud tears welling in them.

"You did it. You did it! I *knew* you'd do it!" Antoni said. "Can I get a ride back, for old time's sake?"

"Let her be, cat. She's exhausted. You can catch a lift on me," Merlin said.

"No thanks, monster guy. I think I'd rather walk," Antoni quipped.

Billie continued down the path toward the farm. Antoni walked beside her. "What a world we live in!" she said. "My friend Billie Someday, born a farm goat, smallest kid on the farm, and she made it to the top of it all!"

Caesar was asleep on the front porch. The farmer had been disappointed in him since the fateful day Billie escaped, and Caesar's world had felt miserable ever since. That was back when he had returned to the farm with Kate but not with the farmer's other prized goat. He was viewed as the worst kind of shepherd dog. He knew in his heart that he did what was best, even though his current life circumstances gave him some doubts. He could see a frenzy was growing among the farm goats, and he lifted his head to see what was happening.

Doctor Sylvia appeared across from the farmhouse porch, looking excited as she poked her head through her fence. "Come quick—it's Billie! She's back!"

Caesar leapt up from the sadness he had been living with since Billie left, and after he jumped into the goats' pen, he ran to the back gate. It was shut, but that didn't stop him from jumping up and down. "Billie! Billie! Billie!" he barked, alternating leaps at the gate and excitement spins.

Peering through the back gate, Billie looked at Kate with a grin. Kate was looking right back at her with the same grin. "Billie Someday, what was it like at the top? I know it had to be awesome!"

"I don't know how to describe it, Kate. I can't tell you everything. This world is too big. It's full of so much greatness, and really, I hope you see it for yourself. There are so many mountains, so many valleys, farms, and forests, so many roads and lakes, and all those places are full of creatures like me with dreams of their own. When I was up there, I could only see my part in the world, and more than anything, it humbled me."

"I hope it wasn't too humbling. Who are your new friends?" Kate asked.

Antoni jumped up on a fence post. "Hello, my name is Marcus Antoni," she said. "I'm a farm cat."

"Not you. I know you," Kate said jovially.

"I'll go get the farmer. You're staying, right, Billie?" Caesar asked.

"Yes, Caesar," Billie said.

"Woooo-hoooo! FARMER! FARMer! FARmer! Farmer! Farmer, Farmer, Farmer!" Caesar cheered over and over again on his way back to the farmhouse.

Teena stepped toward the gate to address little Kate. "Hi, I'm Teena. You have an *amazing* friend! She opened up the *entire* mountain for *all* to be able to climb. Thanks for letting us borrow her!"

"No one borrows Billie Someday. You cannot borrow a heart, and she's all heart. I'm honored to say she's won over mine." Merlin thought about what was about to happen if the dog did its job. "Billie, we'd better get going before your farmer shows up."

"I understand," Billie replied. "Thank you for the escort, everyone."

"Thanks for teaching me a lesson in humility, kid. Maybe I'll live longer and happier having learned it," Merlin said. "You're a true champion, Billie Someday."

"Thank you, Merlin," Billie said.

"Long live Billie Someday!" Merlin yelled to a crowd of rams, ibex, farm goats, a dog, one cat, and the cow.

The herd of rams and ibex joined his decree. "LONG LIVE BILLIE SOMEDAY!"

The farm goats were in shock. This show of respect toward their smallest member—it was the last thing they would have expected.

Merlin turned and disappeared up the hill with a mixed herd of rams and ibex while the farm goats just stared at all the activity in disbelief.

Teena stayed behind. "Is Sappho here?"

Billie's grandmother came forward from the crowd, and Billie introduced her. "Grandma, this is Teena. Teena, this is my grandmother, the storyteller, Sappho. Teena loves stories, Grandma."

189

"She does? Well, you're welcome back anytime to share stories. Maybe you'll tell us the one of how Billie summited the Matterhorn."

"I'd be honored," Teena said. "I should run now. I think your farmer will be here soon."

With a few graceful strides, Teena was well on her way. Just after she disappeared, the farmer approached the back gate to open it. Only Billie Someday was standing on the other side of it now. His prized little goat had finally returned. He rubbed Caesar's head for the first time in a long time. Caesar looked up at him with his tongue out and a smile across his face. Though many dogs do this frequently, it was a rare occasion for the serious Caesar. The farmer looked over the top of the gate at his precious Billie for a moment to see how the adventurer had fared after being gone for so long. She had a limp, he noticed, but she was otherwise still the same Billie he'd always treasured. He opened the gate properly to let her in. He picked her up with an inner joy that seemed to bounce around all inside of himself. No one on the farm had ever seen the farmer look any happier, and he always looked happy. He brought her inside the fence and locked the gate behind her. Billie was home.

Billie looked a little uncomfortable being locked up again, so Caesar said to her, "Don't worry, mate. You can go out again as soon as you'd like. I'll make sure of it."

Satisfied, the farmer walked back to the farmhouse, knowing Billie was safe.

Billie's mother, Edna, came out of the barn after hearing her daughter was home. Billie had wondered how her mother would react after she had tried so hard to keep Billie from getting hurt out there in the world. To Billie's great surprise, she was proud. In fact, Edna was beaming with a pride greater than the pride she'd displayed the day she gave birth to her daughter, Billie. "I'm so proud of you," she told Billie. "You made your dream come true." Edna followed alongside her daughter as Billie walked toward the stable. "What's next, Billie? What's the next adventure? What's your next big stunt? I want to be there for it."

"The next big thing I'm doing is getting some sleep. And, Mother . . . thank you. It means the world that you're proud of me." On her way to the barn, Billie looked over her shoulder at Story Tree Hill. The hill was covered in bright green grass, and the tree was full of life, with all its green summer leaves filling the branches. A gentle breeze gave the tree an extra liveliness by politely asking its leaves to dance for the entirety of its passing through. The sight made Billie grin inside and out.

It may have felt like an ordinary July evening high in the mountain valley, but you can be sure that it was not. This was a special day, because in the valley there happened to be a farm where, on a barn floor of well-trampled hay and mud, lay a champion who had returned home. Because she was exhausted from her incredible adventure, her herd decided to let her have the stable all to herself so she could get much-needed and well-deserved rest. This little farm goat was a champion, and she had earned it.

Sitting quietly by herself in the farm's stable, she was chewing cud and replenishing her energy after completing a feat that no one believed was even possible. They call this little legend Billie Someday, and still to this day, there are so many all over this world that will tell you, she's *the greatest of all time*.

The End

A Sincere Thank You

First and foremost, I would like to thank Clint Greenleaf for coming up with the publishing model many years ago that I've used today to publish Billie. It is one thing to bet on yourself, but it is another to bet on yourself wisely and that's what Clint's model has offered me. Thank you, Clint and to the partners at River Grove.

Thank you to Tanya Hall for overseeing a great staff and all that you do for authors through them. Eleanor Fishbourne and Danny Sandoval: thank you for helping me through the door; you made a difficult decision easier. Ava Justine and Kirstin Andrews: thank you for helping shape *Billie Someday* into the book it became with your edits. Jessica Reyes, Stephanie Mlynarski, Shannon Zuniga, and Tiffany Barrientos: thank you for making this a smooth experience. I really enjoyed working with you.

A special thanks to Cameron Stein and Chase Quarterman for your artwork. You were incredibly easy to work with and your ability to make my vision a reality was an unbelievable experience. Chelsea Richards: your ideas for helping Billie get into the hands of young readers out there was the help I truly needed. Lindsay Bohls: thank you for guiding me along the way and keeping this project on point.

To my wife, Darcie: Thank you for supporting this entire adventure. You were there at the start and with me all the way through. I love you and look forward to tomorrow with you every day.

To all of you, I have a deep profound respect for what you've done for me and I sincerely thank you for it.

About the Author

After spending years adventuring across the planet with a documentary camera, taking part in creating major motion films (including becoming an alternate stunt driver), completing many oil painting compositions, and sailing the open seas in a 34-foot sailboat, Andy Graham has settled into writing about adventures and leaning on his experiences to color the page with black and white text.